TROUBLE ISLAND

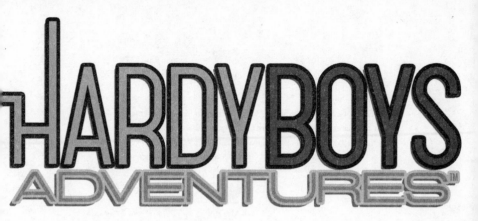

HARDY BOYS ADVENTURES™

#22 *TROUBLE ISLAND*

FRANKLIN W. DIXON

ALADDIN   New York London Toronto Sydney New Delhi

ALADDIN

An imprint of Simon & Schuster Children's Publishing Division

1230 Avenue of the Americas, New York, NY 10020

First Aladdin hardcover edition February 2021

Text copyright © 2021 by Simon & Schuster, Inc.

Cover illustration copyright © 2021 by Kevin Keele

THE HARDY BOYS MYSTERY SERIES, HARDY BOYS ADVENTURES, and related logos are trademarks of Simon & Schuster, Inc.

Also available in an Aladdin paperback edition.

All rights reserved, including the right of reproduction in whole or in part in any form.

ALADDIN and related logo are registered trademarks of Simon & Schuster, Inc.

For information about special discounts for bulk purchases, please contact Simon & Schuster Special Sales at 1-866-506-1949 or business@simonandschuster.com.

The Simon & Schuster Speakers Bureau can bring authors to your live event. For more information or to book an event contact the Simon & Schuster Speakers Bureau at 1-866-248-3049 or visit our website at www.simonspeakers.com.

Series designed by Karin Paprocki

Interior designed by Mike Rosamilia

The text of this book was set in Adobe Carlson Pro.

Manufactured in the United States of America 0121 FFG

2 4 6 8 10 9 7 5 3 1

Library of Congress Cataloging-in-Publication Data

Names: Dixon, Franklin W., author.

Title: Trouble Island / by Franklin W. Dixon. | Description: New York : Aladdin, 2021. | Series: Hardy boys adventures ; 22 | Audience: Ages 8 to 12. | Summary: "A cooking competition goes wrong when a storm traps both the Hardy brothers and a criminal on the small Rubble Island"— Provided by publisher.

Identifiers: LCCN 2020029209 (print) | LCCN 2020029210 (ebook) | ISBN 9781534450240 (pbk) | ISBN 9781534450257 (hc) | ISBN 9781534450264 (ebook)

Subjects: CYAC: Mystery and detective stories. | Brothers—Fiction. | Islands—Fiction.

Classification: LCC PZ7.D644 Tth 2021 (print) | LCC PZ7.D644 (ebook) | DDC [Fic]--dc23

LC record available at https://lccn.loc.gov/2020029209

LC ebook record available at https://lccn.loc.gov/2020029210

CONTENTS

PROLOGUE

JOE

I'M NOT SURE THE LEMON SAUCE THICKENED up as much as it was supposed to," Aunt Trudy murmured, pursing her lips as she stared at the slice of shrimp-asparagus pizza she'd just placed in front of me. "Colton's recipe said you're supposed to *dollop* it on top. But it was more like . . . a drizzle."

Colton, in this case, was Colton Sparks—Aunt Trudy's favorite celebrity chef. He hosts *six*—count 'em, six—different shows on the YUM! Network, and also has five different restaurants across the country. That includes his newest, Spice of Life, which is off Central Park in New York City. We'd brought Aunt Trudy there for her most recent birthday. It had been my idea. She loved it. She even cried a little. It was *way* more successful than last year, when I'd given her a Snuggie. Live and learn.

"I'm sure it's great," my dad said, settling down on the couch with his own helping of pizza. "Everything you make is great, Trudy! You're always so critical of your cooking, when I've never had anything so delicious."

Trudy blushed. "I just want to get it right."

"OMG," my brother Frank announced through a mouthful of shrimp, asparagus, and cheese. "Aunt Trudy, this is your best yet! Well—I guess your crab lasagna was a *little* better."

"Thank you, Frank." She glanced from my brother to the TV set, which was on mute. "Oh! It's starting! Someone hit the button."

My mom grabbed the remote and turned on the sound.

"—come to *Who Gets Cut?*" Colton Sparks was saying to the audience. He was a big, thirtysomething guy with hair so perfectly golden blond that it had to come out of a bottle. He looked like he spent a lot of time in the gym, and he liked to show off his biceps in brightly colored polo shirts embroidered with little versions of the food he was talking about that day on his show. Today his shirt was lime green with a tiny pink shrimp. "This is the game show that asks, who should be sous-chef at Rare, my new steak house in Las Vegas?"

"I can't even imagine," Aunt Trudy said, picking up her own slice of pizza. "I know I can cook, but think what I could learn with some one-on-one time with a master like Colton Sparks! Incredible."

"You might just get that chance, Aunt Trudy," I pointed out.

She quickly shushed me. Colton was speaking again.

"As you know, tonight we have a special announcement. My Home Cooking Masters Seafood Extravaganza invited viewers to send in their best seafood recipes to be judged by me and my team. The person with the best recipe will win a weeklong internship at one of my award-winning restaurants, or ten thousand dollars, but who would choose that?" He paused to wink a blue eye at the camera. "We received some amazing entries, from pot pies to pasta to salads. . . ."

Aunt Trudy put down her pizza and began tapping her fingers on the coffee table. "Oh gosh," she whispered. "Salads! Why didn't I think of that! So fresh and healthy! I'm so nervous! Oh gosh, oh gosh, oh gosh . . ."

Frank's gaze met mine, and I could tell that he, like me, was wondering if we were allowed to speak again.

He decided to risk it. "Aunt Trudy, I can't imagine that—"

"*SHHHHHH!*" Our aunt held up her hand to silence him. Frank looked at me, shrugged, and dug into his pizza again. I'd been too nervous to take a bite up until that point, but now I was hungry, so I followed suit.

Daaaaaaaang. That pizza was amazing—and the lemon sauce was the perfect consistency, of course. Aunt Trudy was a master.

Of course, I already knew that, because about six weeks before, when she was perfecting her crab lasagna recipe to send to Colton Sparks's contest, Frank and I had volunteered to be her taste testers. What followed were several days of tasting more than fifteen different types of crab lasagna. Some had been light, some heavy. Some chewy, some slick. One experiment had blue cheese, a choice that Aunt Trudy, Frank, and I had all agreed was a big mistake. ("It's the pressure, it's getting to me," Aunt Trudy had explained.) But the final recipe we all decided on—a delicate mixture of crab, ricotta and mozzarella cheese, butternut squash, yellow peppers, and the secret ingredient, a sprinkling of gruyère cheese—*that* was a masterpiece.

There was no way Aunt Trudy was not at least placing in this contest.

I tried to concentrate on my pizza while Colton blathered on about what a unique opportunity this internship was and how carefully he and his team had re-created and tasted each and every recipe. Then he spent some time talking about how much he loved his fans, how clever they were, and how they really understood how to "put some *spark* in" their recipes. That's his catchphrase. He says it at least five times during each of his shows.

Then, no kidding, he stopped talking and just stared at the camera for about twenty seconds.

I looked around at my parents, Aunt Trudy, and Frank, wondering if I was missing something. Maybe the broadcast had frozen? Finally, at about second eighteen, I asked, "Is he seriously not going to—"

"*SHHHHHHHHHH!*" Aunt Trudy hissed.

And like magic, just as she finished, Colton started speaking again.

"The winner of this year's Home Cooking Masters Seafood Extravaganza is . . ."

There was a drumroll, and at least ten more seconds before he spoke again, but I'd learned my lesson and wasn't saying another word. Fool me once, etc., etc.

"TRUDY HARDY OF BAYPORT!"

As soon as the name was announced, I heard something shatter. Aunt Trudy had dropped her plate, and it had crashed on the hardwood floor, breaking into a million pieces, sending her pizza skidding toward the TV and leaving a streak of lemon sauce in its wake. Aunt Trudy was just staring at the TV, frozen—stunned.

"Trudy!" shouted my dad. "You won! You did it!"

Frank put down his plate, leaned over, and hugged her. "I knew you would!" he cried. "You always feed us so well!"

Slowly Aunt Trudy's shocked face shifted into a smile. "I did it," she said quietly. "I actually did it!"

I put down my plate and moved over to give her a hug too. "Of course you did. That recipe was perfect!"

She shook her head, as if trying to wake up from a dream. "I'm going to meet Colton Sparks," she said happily. "My idol! I can't wait. I'm going to learn so much."

GONE WITH THE WIND

1

Six months later

FRANK

JUSTIN LI DID NOT LOOK PLEASED.

"So nobody took my money," he said, frowning up at us from the driver's seat of his Mazda 3 in the high school parking lot. The wind started up, icy and mean, making my brother Joe and me hug ourselves and look over longingly at our own car, parked a few rows away. It was that depressing part of spring, before it warms up, when it's just *thinking* about not being winter anymore.

"Well . . . no *human* did," I corrected Justin with a little chuckle. "Is the wind a 'body'? Does it have intention? I guess that's a question for the philosoph—"

"You're saying the wind blew that huge wad of cash off the table at the café, and then into the river?" he said, clearly finding the situation not the least bit funny.

"That *is* what the security footage from the car dealership seemed to reveal," Joe said, lifting up his smartphone for Justin to see. "Would you like to watch it again?"

It had been really hard for us to get that footage, actually, but Justin clearly didn't care. He shook his head, taking on a thousand-yard stare. I glanced at Joe nervously, and his expression confirmed that he too had noticed what I feared: Justin was going to the dark place. Since Justin was six foot four and at least two hundred pounds, this was troubling.

"All my barista money," he muttered, his eyes narrowing as he stared past us. "Over four hundy. Do you know how many lattes I had to make? How many ladies I had to argue with about whether I'd put *enough* vanilla syrup in? That was my guitar money. Do you know how many girls I was going to get with that thing?" When Joe and I didn't respond quickly enough, Justin looked annoyed, like we weren't following. "The *guitar*," he said.

"I can see you're disappointed," I replied, trying to take on the soothing tone my mom uses when she talks me down from a major blow. "But all things considered, isn't it *better* that no human took your money? The wind is a bummer, sure, but it's also a fluke. You don't have to feel all mopey about the vicissitudes of human nature, or anything like that."

Justin looked up at me then. From his scowl and the sharp angle of his eyebrows, it was clear he was irritated. "Vississi-what?" he asked.

"Never mind," Joe said. "Look, Justin, we're really sorry

about your guitar money. Maybe next time, don't carry so much cash around? And definitely don't leave it in an envelope on an outdoor café table on a windy day."

Justin shook his head. "If it was a dude, I could punch him, at least. You can't punch the *wind*."

This is factually untrue, but I decided not to call him on it. He didn't seem to be in the right frame of mind. "I'm really sorry," I said.

Justin sighed, then pulled his long legs into his Mazda. "Well, at least I didn't pay you anything."

"Yeah," Joe said dryly. "At least *that*."

Justin had closed the door and started up the car by then, so if he picked up on Joe's tone, he showed no sign of it. He rolled the window back down an inch. "Thanks, I guess," he said with another sigh before backing out of his parking space and taking off.

Joe and I both watched the spot where Justin's car had been for a few seconds. I don't think either of us really knew what to say.

"That was an anticlimax," Joe finally commented.

"Yeah," I muttered. "Good thing he didn't pay us."

Joe let out a hard snort. "I can't blame him, though. There's nothing satisfying about knowing your guitar money's at the bottom of a muddy river and there's nobody to blame but yourself."

I nodded and started walking to our car. Joe followed. "We've had a lot of cases like that lately, though," I complained. "'The wind took your money.' 'You slipped the note into the wrong locker.' 'Oh, she thought that was her guinea pig.'"

Joe sighed. "So true," he muttered. "We haven't solved a real case since Lookout Key."

After I unlocked the car, we automatically fell into our usual spots, me driving, Joe riding shotgun. I turned the key, and the radio and the heat both sputtered on. The radio was playing the same inescapable Katy Perry song—I swear it had been playing when we'd turned the car off that morning.

"It's like everything's on repeat around here. We need some excitement." I pulled the car out of the spot and drove toward the parking lot exit.

"At least spring break is coming up," Joe pointed out.

He was right. We had next week off.

"Yeah, and we have *such exciting plans*."

Joe glanced at me. "Are you being sarcastic, Frank?"

I nodded. In fact, we had zero plans. "Is it working?"

"No," Joe said bluntly. "Stop it. I'm the sarcastic one."

"Maybe it's time to switch things up," I suggested. "That's what we can work on over spring break."

Joe groaned and looked up at the roof. "Please let something interesting happen before Frank turns into me and I turn into him."

Back at the Hardy ranch, Aunt Trudy was cooking something in a big pot while she watched a rerun of *What's Your Flavor?*, Colton Sparks's spice-identifying game show.

She whacked her spoon against the side of the pot. "It's coriander," she cried as some contestant got buzzed. "Who puts *marjoram* in chili?"

"Fun fact!" I announced, thunking my backpack down on the kitchen table and startling Aunt Trudy. She looked over at me, less than thrilled, but I continued anyway. "Coriander is another name for cilantro, a common herb in Latin American cooking. Some people carry a gene that makes them unable to taste cilantro's fresh, piquant flavor. To them, the herb tastes like soap."

Aunt Trudy sighed. "Of course I know that, Frank. I'm a *home chef.* Now look, you've made me miss the answer."

"It was coriander," Joe said. "That Marta lady got it."

"Hmm," Aunt Trudy murmured, unimpressed. "She struggled with allspice earlier. Anyway, boys, help yourselves to some zucchini bread. I made too much again."

"Ooh!" said Joe, running over to the counter and unwrapping a foil-covered block. "Wow, Aunt Trudy. There are four loaves here. And it's not even zucchini season!"

Trudy nodded absently, focused on her show. "I was noodling with the cinnamon, trying to get the amount right. The one on the left is the best, I think."

Joe looked at the loaf he'd unwrapped, confirming it was the right one, and then sliced off two generous helpings. He ripped a corner off one and popped it into his mouth.

"Oh yeah." He moaned. "This is the best zucchini bread I've ever had!"

"You say that literally every time you eat zucchini bread," I pointed out, grabbing a plate and putting my slice on it.

"It'th alwayth true," Joe replied around a huge bite.

We settled down at the kitchen table as Aunt Trudy's game show wrapped up. When the winner—Lisa, who'd gotten the coriander question wrong—was announced, Aunt Trudy frowned. Lisa had won a lifetime supply of spices, plus a trip to Puerto Vallarta, the perfect place to finally figure out cilantro, I guessed.

"You should go on one of those shows," I blurted, before I remembered how touchy that subject was.

Aunt Trudy looked at me and crossed her arms. "I've already won the only prize I ever wanted from this network," she said with a huff. "And it looks like they're never going to deliver."

"Still no word from Sparks's people?" Joe asked. He'd produced a glass of milk from somewhere and began guzzling it, washing down the zucchini bread he'd hoovered.

Aunt Trudy shook her head. "Oh, plenty of words—but they're always, 'We're sorry, Colton's just too busy'; 'He's opening a restaurant in Santa Fe next week'; 'He's presenting at the Daytime Emmys'; 'It's his Maltipoo's third birthday party.'"

"He's that hard to pin down, huh?" I asked.

Our aunt nodded sadly. "I don't mean to whine. I'm sure it's all true, and good for him. I just really was looking forward to that internship." She shrugged. "But it's been six months already, and there's no hope in sight. I've been thinking that I should just give up and take the cash prize. Ten thousand dollars is nothing to sneeze at."

"You could really deck out your kitchen with ten thousand dollars," Joe pointed out. I realized he was halfway through another slice of zucchini bread.

Aunt Trudy nodded again, looking thoughtful, and then forced a smile. "There *is* a new pasta-making attachment for the mixer I've been wanting."

"With ten thousand dollars, you could take a trip yourself," I suggested. "You know, maybe catch up with Lisa in Puerto Vallarta and teach her about coriander?"

Aunt Trudy gave me a wry smile. "Well, there's the bright side. How are you boys, anyway? I've been dominating the conversation. How was your day?"

Joe groaned, and I made a vague gesture like *better leave that behind us*.

Aunt Trudy laughed. "That good, huh? Well, it's a good thing spring break is coming up."

"Yeah," Joe agreed. "Hey, wanna take us to Puerto Vallarta?"

Aunt Trudy laughed at the same time that the phone began to ring. My parents' landline had one of those old-school, actual-bell rings that made you jump out of your seat and pay attention. Aunt Trudy shot me an apologetic glance and made the *one minute* sign, then grabbed the receiver.

"Hello? Hardy residence."

That was the last time we heard Aunt Trudy speak a complete word for at least five minutes. Her eyes went wide, her jaw dropped, and she began to say "Wha—" and got cut off. She laughed giddily. She shook her head in disbelief.

Joe and I watched this silent telenovela, every so often glancing at each other like, *This is good, right?* or *Should we do something?* as we shoved more zucchini bread into our mouths.

When Aunt Trudy finally spoke again, she was wearing a million-watt smile. "That's . . . amazing," she said. "It *is* rather short notice, but as it happens, I don't have plans next week. If you can just go over how I get there one more time?"

She grabbed a notebook and began jotting down information, nodding, every so often saying, "Yes . . . and where does that leave from?"

I looked at Joe. "Wherever she's going, it sounds a lot more remote than Puerto Vallarta."

Aunt Trudy was nodding again. "A ferry? I see. And no cars allowed. Got it. And is there cell ser— Okay. Yes. Sure. Like a get-away-from-it-all kind of place."

Joe raised an eyebrow.

Aunt Trudy let out a happy sigh. "I'm so grateful for the opportunity. Can I just take the night to discuss it with my family and make plans before committing? Yes . . . Yes. Okay. Absolutely, I can get back to you by ten a.m. tomorrow." She paused. "Thank you. Thank you so much. Okay, goodbye."

She turned away from us to slip the phone back into its cradle. Then she just stood there, letting out the sort of happy sound a teakettle makes right before it boils.

"Aunt Trudy?" I asked. "Is it good news?"

"*Such* good news!" she cried, turning around with a huge grin. "Speak of the devil, boys. Honestly. I just can't believe it. That was Colton Sparks's personal assistant, Gemma."

Joe nodded. "And . . . ?"

She laughed, as though she still couldn't quite believe the conversation she'd just had. "He wants me to get on a plane!" she cried. "Not now. Next week. Colton's apparently hosting the Golden Claw Awards—they're prestigious awards for chefs' achievements in preparing seafood."

"How thrilling," I said.

Joe scowled at me, and it took a moment for me to realize he thought I was trying to be sarcastic again, but I wasn't.

In any case, Aunt Trudy didn't seem to notice. "This year they're holding the awards on a remote island off the coast of Maine—Rubble Island. There's a small inn there called the Sea Spray, where Colton is planning to open a new restaurant. Apparently, he's very taken with the island. According to him, it was farm-to-table out of necessity before farm-to-table was trendy. It's supposed to be very beautiful. Anyway, he wants me to come and be his intern for the week!"

"Wow!" I said.

"That's amazing," Joe said. "It's kind of short notice, though, isn't it?"

"Yes, definitely," Aunt Trudy agreed. "But they're paying all my expenses. I'd fly to Portland, Maine, and they'd pick me up from there. You have to drive to a small town on the coast and take a ferry. . . . Oh, and that's the best part!" She looked excitedly from me to Joe.

"The best part?" I prompted.

Aunt Trudy beamed. "They said I could bring up to four guests! Your father will never take off for that long, and neither will your mother, I'm sure. But I thought—well, the two of you are off school next week, and you were just saying you didn't have any plans. . . ."

I looked over at Joe. He raised his eyebrows. "Hmm . . ."

"What do you think, bro?" I asked. "Do we want to spend spring break eating lobster on a remote island with Colton Sparks?"

Joe grinned. "I can't believe you even have to ask! When do we leave?"

TROUBLE NEAR THE HAPPY CLAM

2

JOE

WELCOME TO PORTLAND! GREETED a big red-and-white banner decorated with lobsters, moose, blueberries, and lighthouses as Frank, Aunt Trudy, and I took the escalator down to baggage claim. Passengers and those there to greet them clustered around a little Dunkin' Donuts kiosk by the door, and I could see snow on the ground just outside the terminal, even though we were well into March.

"Do you know what Maine's slogan is?" Frank asked, glancing up from his phone as we paused in front of the baggage belt.

"'It's freakin' cold'?" I asked, only half-kidding.

"'Land of lighthouses,'" Trudy suggested, smiling.

"Nope." Frank shook his head. "It's 'Vacationland.' It's on their license plates and everything. Kind of weird for the people who live here full-time, huh? Like, don't *I* matter?"

"I think there are a lot of seasonal residents," Aunt Trudy said, watching as the belt began rotating. "At least, that's what Colton said about Rubble Island. The population triples between June and September."

"But not a lot of people there in March?" I guessed.

Trudy nodded. "Ooh, there's my bag."

Frank reached out and grabbed her bright purple duffel before it passed us.

"Colton said the lobstering season begins in March, so the islanders will be busy. But no, there shouldn't be many tourists. Which makes it the perfect time to take over the Sea Spray Inn for his awards banquet."

Since arranging the trip, Aunt Trudy had received a phone call from Colton Sparks himself, so they could go over the plans for the banquet. I'd answered the phone and found him a little gruff, but Trudy said he was just really focused on his food . . . to the point where he "sometimes forgets social niceties." For her sake, I hoped she was right. It would stink to find out your culinary hero is a grouch.

When we had all our bags, we looked around, not sure what to do next.

"Are we supposed to, like . . . rent a car?" Frank asked.

"No." Aunt Trudy shook her head. "Colton was very clear that his assistant would pick us up here and take us to his hotel."

"I hope it's a nice hotel," I put in. "I hope they have a hot tub."

Frank sighed. "I just hope Colton's assistant comes soon. It's cold in here. And I could use a rest."

I pointed at the Dunkin' Donuts. "Maybe we should get a coffee? You know, when in Rome."

The line was still at least five people long. But I do love a good French cruller.

Before we could head in that direction, a harried-looking young blond woman entered through a huge revolving door. She took one quick look around baggage claim—filled with people in thick rubber boots and L.L.Bean parkas—and then zeroed in on us Hardys, underdressed in our regular old jackets and sneakers. She lifted a sign hesitantly: TRUDY HARDY AND GUESTS.

"That's us!" Frank said happily.

The woman looked relieved as we walked over. "Oh, I'm so glad," she said, reaching out a hand to Aunt Trudy. Our aunt took it and shook. "I'm Gemma Loreto, Colton's assistant. I'm sorry I'm a little late picking you up. There was a crisis with the sunchoke supplier, and it took longer than I expected to sort out."

"What's a sunchoke?" I asked.

She turned to me, eyes widening. "Are you kidding?"

"Yes," I said, smiling like, *silly me!* I hadn't been, but whatever.

As Gemma led us outside, Aunt Trudy grabbed my arm and pulled me close. "It's a root vegetable related to the sunflower," she whispered. "Kind of like a potato meets a water chestnut? Very delicious roasted."

"What's a water chestnut?" I asked.

Trudy swatted me. "You're hopeless," she hissed.

Before I could reply, our attention was drawn to the vehicle Gemma seemed to be leading us toward—a long black stretch limousine. She paused by the passenger door.

"Are you serious?" asked Frank.

Gemma looked back, surprised. "Oh, the limo? Standard request for Colton. And since you'll be traveling with him, well, you'll be traveling in style." She gestured to the driver, who got out and opened the trunk, then took our luggage.

"Come on," Gemma said, waving us over. "And make yourselves comfortable."

We did. Soon we were driving out of the airport and turned onto the highway. We passed a couple of exits before taking the one for downtown Portland. Downtown was filled with old brick buildings, all pitched down a sloping hill toward the harbor. We stopped in front of one of the largest and grandest.

"This is Colton's hotel," Gemma said. "We'll meet him here and then drive over to catch the boat to Rubble Island."

When she climbed out, I turned to Aunt Trudy and Frank. "I guess we're not staying here, then."

Aunt Trudy shrugged. "I wasn't completely clear on our itinerary once we got to Portland. But we'll get to Rubble Island and have time to get the lay of the land."

I realized Gemma wasn't waiting for us, so we left our luggage and hopped out of the limo, following her up the imposing front steps, through a golden-lit lobby, and into an elevator. Gemma slid her key card into a slot and pressed *P*.

"Penthouse," Frank whispered to me.

"Right there with you," I whispered back.

When the doors started to open, we could immediately hear raised voices.

"I don't care whether you *tried* or not!" a male voice was shouting. Colton. "Will there or will there not be fresh truffles waiting for me? And *do not* tell me I can just use oil. . . ."

The elevator doors had fully opened, and Gemma stepped out into what looked like a shared sitting room. A few doors opened off different walls, I guessed to different bedrooms. Aunt Trudy, Frank, and I stood in the elevator, slack-jawed and awkward, until Gemma cleared her throat loudly and gestured for us to hurry out.

Colton stopped in the middle of his sentence and turned to stare at us with wide blue eyes. He was wearing a baby-blue polo shirt with what looked like a rare steak on the chest. He was really pretty huge in person, and more than a little intimidating. Soon the eyes of the other two men in the room swung toward us too.

"Who are these people?" Colton asked sharply, frowning at Gemma.

She responded by turning her smile up to eleven. *"Colton!"* she said playfully. "Don't be *silly*! Ha, ha! You remember Trudy Hardy, the winner of your most recent *Who Gets Cut?* contest!"

Colton's eyes passed over me, then Frank, and then settled on Trudy. "Uh-huh," he said simply.

I wouldn't have thought it possible, but Gemma pushed her smile up to twelve. "Colton! Come on, say hello! I know Trudy is excited to finally meet you in person."

Aunt Trudy actually looked a little less excited than she had a moment ago. She doesn't suffer fools, honestly, and I was beginning to wonder how this week was going to go for her. But Colton fastened his eyes on hers, donned his most charming smile, and walked over to us, hand extended. "It's very nice to meet you at last, Trudy. I could tell just speaking to you on the phone that we'll learn a lot from each other."

Trudy chuckled. "Oh, don't be silly! I'm sure I'll learn more from—"

Colton suddenly held up his hand, then pointed a less-than-enthusiastic finger at me and Frank. "Who are these two?" he asked.

"I'm Joe!" I blurted eagerly, because I can read a room.

Frank laughed nervously. "And I'm Frank. We're Trudy's nephews."

"Nephews?" Colton asked, turning to Gemma and narrowing his eyes. "I'm sorry, what was that contest called again? 'Win an internship with Colton for you and six of your favorite nephews'?"

"There are two of us," Frank said, unnecessarily.

Gemma held up a finger. "Actually, Colton," she said in an even voice, "I'm sure you'll recall that we offered to pay for up to four guests for Miss Hardy—because of the short notice, and the amount of travel required."

Colton stared at Gemma, seeming to take this in. As an amateur detective, I notice things. And I was noticing two things about this interaction. One, Gemma did not suffer fools either, despite Colton's occasional gruffness. And two, Colton actually listened to her.

He suddenly raised his arm and looked pointedly at his watch. *"Goodness,"* he said. "Two o'clock already! I suppose the car is waiting to take us to our boat?"

Gemma smiled. "Of course, Colton."

His eyes traveled back over to Frank and me. "I trust you'll be sharing a room," he said quietly. "And keeping out of the way. We didn't tell the innkeeper we'd be bringing so many of our closest friends."

I nodded, sensing that we'd won. "Of course," I said. "Frank and I know how to stay out of trouble." *Sort of. Depending on your definition of* trouble. . . .

"Excellent." Colton clapped his hands together. "Let's be on our way, then. Island living awaits!"

"Are there any more peanuts?" Frank hissed at me as the limo turned off onto a yet narrower road for, like, the twentieth time. Maine looks small on a map, but it's apparently pretty huge and the coastline looks like someone's grandma crocheted the most complicated lace she could think of, with endless dips, loops, and scallops. Countless rocky peninsulas jutted out into the ocean as we drove through harbor town after harbor town, many with seafood shacks advertising their "award-winning" lobster rolls. My mouth watered at the sight of every one of them, and given how quickly Frank was destroying the teeny packets of peanuts scattered around the limo, his was too. We hadn't had time to grab lunch at the hotel. Aunt Trudy was busy staring out the windows with a dreamy expression on her face, so I couldn't tell if she was hungry.

Frank dug into his backpack and pulled out the brochure he'd printed out back at home. "Rubble Island sounds like a unique place, huh?" he said loudly, glancing over at Colton, who was on the bench facing us, buried in his tablet. He glanced up at Frank, gave a curt nod, and looked back down at the screen.

"Rubble Island is a very interesting place," Gemma put in, smiling big enough to make up for Colton's glowering. "It's an old, remote lobstering community about ten miles off the Maine coast. There's a historic hotel there—the Sea Spray Inn, where we'll be staying. The island population triples during the summer, though services are too limited for most casual tourists."

Colton coughed. "That's certainly true. At present. Unfortunately, the locals aren't terribly friendly."

Aunt Trudy glanced over from the window. "Oh, surely that's not true?"

Frank nodded. "To be generous, maybe they just don't want the island overrun. It looks like a stunningly beautiful spot. And most of it's protected land?"

"Yes," Gemma answered. "There are several hiking trails through the preserve, though."

"Don't worry," Colton added, still staring at his screen. "We won't be dealing with the locals much. I've designed our trip so that once the other chefs arrive, we'll only be socializing with them."

His attention returned to whatever he was reading, and when Aunt Trudy and Gemma fell silent too, Frank flipped through his printout one more time before putting it away.

I nudged him, then shook three peanuts out of the bag I was holding. "This is it," I whispered. "I'll split them with you."

Frank sighed. "We have to be there soon, right?" he whispered.

"I think so." I checked my watch again. "We've been on the road for about an hour."

Just then the woods on either side of the narrow road

opened up to reveal a hill and, at the bottom, a bunch of small buildings clustered around a pier. We passed several cottage-size colonial houses, a couple of which looked like they might be stores or restaurants during the summer season, but which were closed up now. Near the pier were a couple of brick buildings, and as we got closer, I saw signs out front that labeled them a general store and a bed-and-breakfast.

I glanced over at Gemma. "Is this . . . ?"

She nodded. "East Harbor." She raised her arms above her head in a stretch, then glanced over at Colton. To my surprise, the two men he'd been berating when we'd met him at the hotel hadn't joined us in the limo. Before we'd left, Gemma had explained that they were Colton's assistants at his Boston restaurant, Flambé, and were needed back in the kitchen. He'd hired some people to help in the kitchen of the restaurant at the Sea Spray Inn—the Salty Duck—where the Golden Claw Awards were being held, but for the most part, he and our aunt would be in charge of the dinner. Gemma had said it was an "excellent chance to learn," but Aunt Trudy had gone a little pale upon realizing how much responsibility she'd have.

"I guess this really will be a working vacation," she'd whispered to Frank and me as we'd hustled back into the limo.

"Don't worry," I'd replied, squeezing her hand. "You've got this. And we'll help in any way we can."

Now the limo wound through the narrow streets, down

the hill, and parked on the long wooden pier jutting out into the harbor just outside the general store. There wasn't a soul in sight, but a medium-size yacht was waiting at the dock.

"Colton's hired a private craft to take us to Rubble Island, along with his most necessary ingredients," Gemma explained.

"There's a ferry, though, isn't there?" Frank asked.

Colton opened the door closest to him and was climbing out. Gemma glanced quickly from Frank to Colton and back, then lowered her voice. "Colton doesn't like the ferry much. Too many *people*."

"That's funny," I said. "I can't imagine the ferry's that big?"

She looked over at me and clarified, "Oh. I didn't mean too *many* people. I meant too many . . . *people*."

Huh. Before I could digest that, she followed Colton out of the limo. Aunt Trudy, Frank, and I all exchanged looks. Finally Aunt Trudy shrugged and began scooting toward the door. We both followed her.

By the time we got outside, Colton was nearly on the yacht.

"Hey!" I yelled, looking back at the general store. I couldn't help noticing the sign out front: TRY OUR AWARD-WINNING LOBSTER ROLL. BEST IN MAINE. *"Hey!"*

Colton started and turned around, his lips pursed. "Yes? Can I help you, my uninvited guest?"

Gemma shot us an apologetic look, but I was far too hungry to be offended. "Can we stop at the general store for a minute? I could use a rest stop, and I'd love to pick up some lunch."

Colton groaned. "They haven't *eaten*?" he asked, shooting Gemma an accusatory look.

"We didn't have time," she replied simply. "Sure, Joe, the three of you can run into the store. Just . . . make it quick, okay? The sun goes down early at this time of year, and we want to make sure we're settled at the inn before it gets dark."

That sounded vaguely ominous, but I decided not to dwell on it—I guessed a tiny Maine island probably didn't have many streetlights. And anyway, I was too excited to eat my first lobster roll to care. "Great! Be back in a sec."

Aunt Trudy grabbed my arm. "I'm going to stay out here and try to chat with Colton. Okay, boys? But can you get me a sandwich?"

I pointed to the BEST IN MAINE sign. "A *sandwich*? Are you sure?"

She laughed. "Oh, okay. I do love a good lobster roll. Extra butter, please."

"You got it."

I nodded at Frank, and the two of us headed around the building to the store's entrance.

The ground was muddy and wet, and the sky was gray, but you could see how East Harbor could be a really charming town in the summer. A narrow main street wound between the two old brick commercial buildings, one of which bore the date 1897 alongside a sign for THE PLUCKY SEAL B&B. A ramshackle wooden building sat alongside the general store—THE HAPPY CLAM PUB according to the hand-painted sign, although the windows were too dark to tell whether it was open.

Warm golden light spilled from inside the general store's wide windows, and glancing inside, we could see that it was full of people. *So this is where East Harbor hangs out,* I thought.

When we pushed open the front door and stepped in, though, every conversation seemed to come to a halt. The place went from lively-bordering-on-raucous to totally silent. There were about twenty people inside, all decked out in some combination of jeans, flannel, and fleece.

They were all staring at us.

"Um," I said, looking at the collection of largely gray-haired men and women sitting around a narrow sandwich bar and at two picnic-style tables. None of them looked happy about our arrival. "Is there a bathroom in here?"

Silently, five or six of them pointed to the back of the store. I nodded my thanks, and Frank and I plowed in that direction, relieved to find an empty men's room behind the beer fridge.

"What *was* that?" Frank asked as we went about our business.

"I'm not sure," I said honestly. "Maybe it's what Colton was getting at—the locals don't like outsiders?"

"I thought that was on the island. And how do they know we're outsiders?"

I snorted. I didn't often get the opportunity to explain logic to my oh-so-rational brother. "Frank, look at the size of this town. How many people do you think live here?"

"Oh." He sighed. "What do we do?"

"I don't know what you're doing," I replied, going over to the sink to wash my hands, "but I'm starving. I'm ordering a lobster roll."

Maybe I was imagining it, but the tension seemed just a *bit* lighter as we walked over to the lunch counter. Still, I felt every eye on me as I got the attention of the clerk, a big older guy with bushy gray eyebrows wearing a red plaid flannel shirt. "Uh, hi."

He leaned an elbow on the counter but didn't say anything—he just nodded.

When I get nervous, I tend to get kind of chatty, and this time was no exception. "I'm Joe Hardy, and this is my brother, Frank. We're visiting the area, and wow, this place is so beautiful! You are all so lucky, getting to take this in every day." I gestured to the back of the store, hoping he'd get that I was talking about the harbor beyond.

Everyone else in the store was silent, listening, but only the clerk nodded. He raised an eyebrow. "Ayuh. Some of us wonder why you'd live anywhere else."

I heard some chuckles behind me and let out a nervous laugh. "Yeah, seriously."

The laughter died down, and the silence grew uncomfortable again. The clerk nodded again, like he was encouraging a small child. "Did you want somethin'?"

"Yes!" I cried, suddenly remembering my mission. "Can I get three lobster rolls to go, please? One with extra butter?"

He frowned. "Extra butter? All right. Anything else?"

I shook my head. "That's it. Thanks." As the clerk turned and got out three old-fashioned hot dog rolls, then buttered the sides and slid them on the grill, I could feel the stares of the other customers. I worried that I'd start blurting out more random info any minute. *Do these people want to hear about my midterms?*

"You staying at the Plucky Seal?" the clerk asked suddenly, flipping the hot dog buns to grill the other side. "Abigail didn't mention you."

"Oh, no," Frank said. He was standing awkwardly about five feet behind me, hands in his pockets, rocking on his heels like he does when he's feeling out of his element. "We're, ah, we're about to head for Rubble Island. I hear it's really—"

The clerk whirled around, nearly flapping the tail of his flannel shirt onto the grill. "Rubble Island?" he asked curiously. "What takes you out there? The ferry won't be leaving until the morning."

"Actually," I said, "we're going by private boat."

"Well, la-di-da," he said.

"I mean, we're not paying for it," I blurted. "We're actually here with Colton Sparks. Do you know him? He's the YUM! Network guy. You know—'I'm sorry, your cooking is a massive failure, and you're *CUT*!' *Zzzzzzing*." I sliced my hand through the air like the graphic of a knife that always accompanied the famous tagline.

The clerk stared at me, zero warmth on his face. "I know who Colton Sparks is," he replied in a growl, then spun around, pulled a big plastic container of seafood out of a small fridge, and began piling up the hot dog rolls with lobster meat. When he was done, he made a big show of turning back around to me, scowling, and dribbling extra melted butter from a small ceramic pitcher onto the last one. "Like that?" he asked.

"Yeah," I said, somehow feeling ashamed. "That's, uh . . . fine."

He wrapped each roll in waxed paper, took my cash, then pushed them across the counter without another word.

"Thanks," I said, but he'd already turned back to the grill to clean it.

Every eye in the store still seemed to be on me, but the mood had changed. Whereas the locals had originally seemed curious—with maybe a *touch* of bemusement—now it felt like their expressions were outright hostile. Several people were scowling, and as I made my way back to Frank, a few of them huffed before turning away.

I was almost at the door, already looking forward to getting out of the place, when the clerk's voice suddenly boomed toward me again: "That Colton Sparks . . . is he out there now?"

I hesitated, then glanced at Frank. I could tell he wasn't sure what to do either. Colton was a celebrity, and I didn't want to put him in a weird position by announcing his location to a packed café. He probably got approached by people he didn't really want to talk to all day long. But at the same time, I couldn't really deny Colton was there, since I'd *just* said we were getting on his boat.

"Um, yeah," I finally said.

The clerk straightened up like a toy soldier and threw down the rag he'd been using to clean. He marched out from behind the counter, past us, and onto the main street, and then toward the pier.

"Uh-oh," Frank muttered.

"What do you think he's going to do?"

Frank nodded past me. "Only one way to find out." Right. I darted out the door and ran after the clerk, Frank hot on my heels. Behind us, some of the customers from the general store were following a little more slowly.

We rounded the building just in time to see the clerk running to the end of the pier where the yacht was docked. Colton, Gemma, and Aunt Trudy were all sitting on a narrow plastic chest, chatting and laughing.

The clerk ran right up to them and poked his finger into Colton's stunned face. I caught up just in time to hear him growl, "You're not welcome here!"

Shock—even fear—flickered in Colton's eyes, but it lasted less than a second. He stood up, jutting his chin into the air, and looked down his nose at the man. "That's fine. We're just leaving." He gestured to Gemma and Aunt Trudy, who hurriedly got up, grabbed their things, and started down the gangplank to the boat.

"Not fast enough," the clerk replied. "You know, I got some good friends on Rubble Island. If it were up to me, you wouldn't be welcome there, either."

Colton rolled his eyes and huffed. "Well, it's a good thing you're not in charge, then." He glanced in our direction. "Get on the boat, boys."

I wasn't about to argue. Frank and I scurried down the gangplank. As soon as our feet hit the deck, we heard the yacht's engine start up. Colton was right behind us. A deckhand, a guy not much older than Frank, appeared from the cabin and pulled the gangplank back onto the boat. We exchanged a nod, but my attention quickly cut back to the man on the pier.

As we pulled away, he reared back and spit in our direction, and the other general store customers who'd followed us onto the pier cheered.

The boat was moving faster now, and soon the pier and then the whole harbor retreated into miniature. Still, no one aboard said anything. I looked from Frank to Aunt Trudy: *What the—?*

"Well," Colton said as the yacht charged toward the open ocean, "I guess he was a Paolo Vasquez fan."

We all laughed uncomfortably. Paolo Vasquez was the host of *Spice Roulette*, the second-most-popular show on the YUM! Network. He and Colton had a rivalry that always seemed kind of staged to me.

I looked over at Frank. We locked eyes, and I could tell my brother was thinking the same thing I was: *That seemed a lot more personal than just not being a fan.*

FRANK

OW," AUNT TRUDY MURMURED APPRE-
ciatively as the yacht sailed past Heron
Rock and Seal Rock, the two tiny islands
that Gemma had said marked the entrance
to Rubble Island's harbor. "I knew it would
be beautiful, but I couldn't have imagined this."

Each of the smaller islands was made up of granite
cliffs fringed by long wild grass, with tiny spruce forests
rising from the rock. The sun was dipping low in the
sky—Gemma explained that sunset here was about half
an hour earlier than we were used to—and it cast a gorgeous pinky-gold light over the islands and the rolling
sea. The sky was a vibrant violet blue, with a few silver-
tinged puffy clouds.

"This is pretty special," Joe agreed. "I can see why people make the effort to come out here."

Once we were past Heron and Seal Rocks, Rubble Island spread out before us. It was small—about five square miles, Colton had said—rocky and forested on one half and full of grassy fields on the other. As we drew closer to the pier, we could see sheep and goats grazing. The island's many hills were dotted with modest wooden houses, some more like cabins than year-round dwellings. There was also a lighthouse poking out from a high rise and a small, clearly old, white schoolhouse a little farther along.

The Sea Spray Inn took up most of the land facing the pier. Gemma had told us it dated back to the early 1900s. It was long and rectangular, with weathered gray wood shingles, multipaned rectangular windows, and a gabled roof. Two blocky outbuildings, both made of the same weathered wood, sat to the right of the main building. It looked like there was a tiny porch on the very top of the main building's roof. I remembered from my research it was called a widow's walk. The wife of a sailor might have stood up there, looking hopefully for his ship to return to port. Even from a distance, I could see some tables set up on the inn's wide covered porch.

"Does it look small to you?" Joe whispered, sidling up beside me at the deck's railing.

"The restaurant, the Salty Duck?" I asked, and he nodded. "Kind of. It's a weird place to hold this big awards presentation."

Someone cleared his throat right behind us, and I started. Colton was gazing at the inn and restaurant. "Actually, the Salty Duck's chef, Polly Hopkins, is a close friend and a pioneer in farm-to-table dining. I know the chefs coming for the Golden Claw Awards will fall in love with Rubble Island, just like I have!"

Before we could respond, he walked over to where the deckhand we'd seen before was setting up the gangplank. It looked like we were almost ready to disembark.

I took a deep breath of fresh sea air as I stepped onto the fishing pier. A few fishermen in waterproof overalls were unloading their boats onto a pickup truck nearby, but they took one glance at our group, scowled, and looked away.

I nudged Joe. "Did you see that?"

"How they just kind of scowled at us? Yeah."

"Do you think we're going to be seen as the enemy here? Like, how much can one island hate a celebrity chef? I know some people say *Who Gets Cut?* is rigged, but . . ."

"It's not *rigged*," Joe replied. "It's just that anyone who tries to sous vide anything gets bounced. But really, they should know better."

Aunt Trudy clucked behind him. "So true, Joe. Sous vide is the *worst*. What you gain in flavor, you lose in texture."

One of the fishermen seemed to overhear and glared at us.

"You saw that, right?" I hissed at Joe.

"Yep."

As we left the pier, I could feel the eyes of the fishermen

on us. And I couldn't help wondering whether their chilly reception had something to do with what the cashier had said (and spat) in East Harbor. Was *anyone* happy to see Colton Sparks on Rubble Island?

As we caught up to Colton, we could hear him complaining again. "Where's my truck?"

"Wait, I thought cars weren't allowed on the island," I said before I thought better of it. Colton looked at me like he'd been unpleasantly reminded that I could talk. "I mean, the fishermen have one. But—I thought—"

"There are very few cars on the island," Colton agreed. "And they're very strict about who can own one. In fact, you have to have a disability to even bring a golf cart here. Someone was supposed to bring a truck to the pier for us to unload our things. Clearly, they forgot."

I glanced up at the inn, then back at the yacht. The crew had already brought up several coolers and a pallet of ingredients. It didn't seem like stuff we could easily hoof up the hill. "Uhhh . . ."

"It's fine," Colton said crisply. "We'll just have to walk to the inn to remind them. For now, you boys and Trudy should carry your luggage."

I glanced at Joe. *Good thing we packed light.* That "How to Plan a Capsule Wardrobe for Your Vacation to a Remote New England Island" pin that Joe had found on Pinterest had really helped. I grabbed Aunt Trudy's roller suitcase and nodded her on. "Don't worry. We've got this."

The gravel road that led up the hill to the inn was mostly deserted, but a few people were standing around in front of what looked like a coffee shop. An older woman was perusing flyers at a wooden bulletin board next to the ferry ticket office. Maybe I was just getting paranoid, but I swore I could feel their unfriendly eyes on us as we passed by. I wasn't sure I'd ever been on a vacation where everyone at the destination hated me. That seemed like a bad marketing plan on the part of the resort.

At the top of the hill, we turned right onto a dirt path that led through a pretty rock garden up to the wide covered porch. Double doors framed by windows were labeled RECEPTION. "Jacques? Are you there?" Colton called as he led the way inside.

As we all trooped into the elegant lobby, I took in dark hardwood floors, cream-colored walls, and an old-fashioned reception desk that looked like it might have been there since the early 1900s. A tall, thin, middle-aged man with dark hair and a neat beard strode in from an adjoining room. "Colton!" he cried warmly.

Colton moved forward and embraced the man. When they parted, he turned to introduce us. "Everyone, this is my dear friend, and the owner of the Sea Spray Inn, Jacques Lemont."

"Welcome, welcome." As Jacques spoke, I could hear the shadow of a French accent. And then I noticed that the lobby smelled *amazing*—like roasted meat, garlic, and delicate spices. My stomach growled. The lobster roll had been tasty, but the sea had tossed us back and forth so much on the ride over, it had been hard to enjoy it.

Jacques looked at us, smiling. "Gemma, it's good to see you again."

"Same to you," she replied with a smile. "We're all very happy to be here. Let me introduce . . ."

Gemma went around the room. If the innkeeper was surprised that Joe and I had been added to the guest list, he showed no hint of it. "I'm so pleased you all could make it and that you'll have the opportunity to see some of the island. Please join me in the Salty Duck for dinner."

He opened a glass-paned door that led into an adjoining room. Inside, we found a cozy dark-walled dining room with heavy wood furniture and a blazing fireplace on the far wall. Spring had yet to take the chill out of the air, so the warmth felt amazing.

"This place is so lovely!" Aunt Trudy said, looking around appreciatively.

"Thank you so much," a voice called, and then suddenly a door on the wall with the fireplace swung open and an older woman stepped out, smiling. She had warm hazel eyes and steel-gray hair cut into a straight bob. "I'm Polly. Welcome to the Salty Duck! Oh, Colton!" She ran forward and embraced him warmly. "Where is she? Where is your assistant chef who won the contest?"

Colton leaned back and introduced Aunt Trudy. "She

simply *blew me away* with her recipe for crab lasagna," he explained. "And I knew after speaking to her on the phone that I had a true gourmet on my hands."

Aunt Trudy blushed. "Oh, *you*," she said, swatting at Colton, but he only chuckled. "You'll see," she said, turning to Polly. "When we're all working together in the kitchen, I'm going to have a hard time living up to that introduction! I'm really just a humble home chef who loves food."

Polly nodded. "I don't doubt it, but I know how hard it is to impress Colton. And from what I've heard, you *really* impressed him." She paused. "Although I'm afraid I won't be in the kitchen with you. I have a family obligation in Massachusetts that unfortunately can't be postponed. . . . I'll leave tomorrow morning."

"Oh," our aunt said, looking from Polly to Colton. I could tell she was disappointed not to get to work with Polly, but she seemed to also be mentally calculating how much help they'd have in the kitchen. So far, it was Colton and Aunt Trudy . . . plus an undetermined number of local helpers. Would there really be enough hands to pull this meal off?

"The good news," said Polly, "is that while I'm gone, you two will have full run of the kitchen! Let me show you."

She led us through the swinging door and into her beautiful, state-of-the-art kitchen. Aunt Trudy excitedly pointed out every expensive accessory and every unusual feature of the ovens, though most of it went over Joe's and my heads.

It was clear that, help or no, she was going to be very, very happy here.

"You must be starving," Jacques finally said. "Let's eat!"

A few hours later I discreetly reached down and unbuttoned my pants as I settled back in my chair. My flannel shirt provided sufficient cover, and I was *stuffed*. Pomegranate salad with oranges and blue cheese, butternut squash bisque, roast lamb with goat cheese, mashed potatoes and fennel, and a chocolate cherry torte for dessert. The meal had been truly amazing.

As everyone sighed appreciatively, Polly rested her elbows on the table and leaned forward. "Would you believe most of what you just consumed was grown here on Rubble Island?"

"It was?" Joe asked. "That's impressive. But how?"

"Well, there's a big community garden where the inn tends a plot," Polly explained, "and there's also a greenhouse for off-season gardening. Farm-to-table may be trendy now, but on Rubble Island it's a necessity. Without it, it would be difficult to get high-quality fresh vegetables here, especially in the winter."

"What a great solution," Aunt Trudy mused, and then a yawn slipped out. "Oh, excuse me! How rude!"

"No, not at all!" said Jacques. "You've had a long day. You must be exhausted."

While we tried to shake our heads politely, Jacques wasn't wrong. We'd had to get up really early for our flight. Arriving at the Portland airport seemed like it had happened a million years ago. Now that I was full of delicious food, I could feel my eyelids getting heavy.

"I am a little tired," Colton agreed. "Perhaps we should get our rest. Trudy and I have to be up early tomorrow so we can get to work! Come, Trudy—I believe the food from the dock has been delivered. Let me show you what we'll be working with." He led her into the kitchen. When they returned a few minutes later, Aunt Trudy looked a little bewildered.

"*How* many people will be working with us?" she asked Colton.

He waved his hand dismissively. "Oh, don't worry. We'll have a few extra hands. But really, I want to use the awards banquet as an opportunity to teach you everything I know! Aren't you lucky?"

I caught Joe's eye. *Lucky,* I mouthed. He shook his head and mouthed back, *Is he serious?*

Polly pushed away from the table. "Jacques, show these exhausted people to their rooms," she said with a grin. "I'll clean up here."

"Oh, no, Polly," Aunt Trudy protested. "You made us such a wonderful meal! I can—"

"Don't be silly. I don't have an early flight tomorrow, and I didn't spend all day on a plane, then a car, then a boat. Go up to your rooms and get some rest. It's been a real pleasure to host you all."

We thanked her, and after a few minutes, Jacques led us back into the lobby and grabbed some keys from behind the reception desk. "Come on," he said. "I'll show each of you to your rooms."

As we sleepily followed Jacques up the stairs, a terrible thought occurred to me. "Hey," I said, trying to sound casual. "I sort of remember from my brochures that not all the rooms have electricity?"

Jacques laughed. "Oh, yes—that's true. This inn dates back to 1916. Did you know that?"

"I, uh . . . I read something like that," I replied. But what I was thinking was, *Old things are cool and all that, but I was really hoping to charge my phone. . . .*

"Some of the summer guests don't mind—they come to Rubble Island to get away from it all," Jacques went on. "But your party will be staying in the main building, where all the rooms have full amenities. The outbuildings are closed up for the season. We don't get many guests in March."

Phew!

"Are there any other guests here now?" Joe asked.

Jacques nodded. "Only two right now. It'll be very quiet."

We'd arrived on the second floor, where a long hallway with a plush red carpet led past a series of ten or so rooms. Jacques guided us to a door on the right. "This will be you, Frank and Joe—I hope you don't mind sharing? The inn is mostly in hibernation mode at this time of year, and when Gemma sent word that you'd be coming, I wanted to make sure your room had time to warm up. If you need separate rooms, I can have one prepared tomorrow."

"This is fine," Joe said with a sleepy grin. "If it has beds in it, I'm sold."

Jacques laughed. "Two beds, in fact! What luxury."

He pushed open the door and we walked through a narrow foyer into a charming wood-paneled space with two double beds, each covered in a puffy white duvet. On the far end of the room, two windows looked out into the darkness. It was hard to tell what our view was, but I was excited to find out in the morning.

"This is perfect," I said sincerely. "Thank you for having us."

"It's my pleasure," Jacques said, retreating to the door. We called our good nights to Aunt Trudy, Colton, and Gemma, and then Jacques pulled the door closed behind him.

We didn't take long getting into our pj's, brushing our teeth, and climbing beneath those cozy cream-colored duvets. The bed was soft and warm, and the pillows were excellent. Joe clicked off the lamp. "Good night, Frank."

"Night."

After a few seconds, I chuckled. "Do you hear that?"

"What?"

"The waves." I was quiet so that Joe could listen to the water slapping against the rocky shore.

"Oh, wow. We must be really close to the ocean!"

"I know. I can't wait to explo—"

But I never finished what I was saying, because right at that moment, we heard a loud crash, followed by a bloodcurdling scream. Joe flicked on the light, and we stared at each other in alarm and spoke at the same time:

"*Aunt Trudy?*"

PETTY SQUABBLES
4

JOE

I N SECONDS FRANK AND I HAD TOSSED OFF OUR covers and jumped to our feet. Frank threw open the door and we raced out into the hallway. A little farther down the hall, our aunt emerged dressed in her bathrobe, looking just as concerned as we were.

"Who was that?" she asked. "I heard someone scream."

"Me too!" I cried.

A few seconds later, a third door opened, and Gemma, still in her street clothes, stepped into the hallway. "Are you all okay?" she asked. "That sounded like Colton."

"Colton?" Frank asked, sounding puzzled. "That's funny. I thought it was a woman."

Gemma was already leading the way to the end of the

hall. "Colton has a very high-pitched scream," she said mildly. I didn't ask how she knew that.

With the three of us close on her heels, Gemma knocked briskly on the door of room 208. "Colton? Is everything all right?" she called.

There was no answer, but we could hear someone moving around inside.

"*Colton?*" Gemma shouted in a louder voice. "We're worried about you. I need to know—"

Thunk. Suddenly the door was yanked open, and Gemma lurched forward. Colton, standing on the other side in a plaid bathrobe, caught her. Behind him was a room bathed in golden light. But from the small amount of bed and rug we could see, nothing appeared out of place.

"Colton," Gemma said again, recovering quickly and getting back to her feet. "Is everything okay? We heard a crash."

He shook his head, his eyes slightly glazed. "Well—it's— I just—"

I glanced at Frank, and we pushed past him into the room. Something had clearly happened—maybe something dangerous—and I was losing patience. The crash had been too loud to be a lamp falling off a table or a glass breaking. It had sounded heavy, almost like a body falling to the floor.

"Oh my gosh," Frank muttered. Over the antique-looking desk, which faced the huge king-size bed, was a large bay window, with its central pane shattered, like something small but heavy had been thrown through it. Now that we were closer, we could hear the waves pounding the rocks outside.

I spun around to face the bed, and there it was, right on the edge, ringed with tiny glass shards.

"Someone threw a brick through your window," I said, stating the obvious, just as Jacques appeared.

"Are you okay?" he asked. "I heard a— Goodness!"

Colton held up his hands. "It's fine! Or I should say, *I'm* fine. I'm sorry, Jacques."

Why is Colton apologizing to Jacques? But before I could ask, Jacques pushed his way into the room and came over to investigate the window.

"Oh my," he said. "Did it hit you?"

"No, no," Colton replied. "It startled me. Some of you probably heard me yell. I was lying in bed at the time. I felt the brick hit the foot of the mattress, but it didn't make contact with me."

Jacques looked from the window to Colton, then shook his head. Without another word, he ran out of the room and down the hallway.

"What's he doing?" Frank asked.

"Who cares?" I replied. "Come on, Frank. Let's follow him."

Before anyone could object, I ran out of the room just in time to see Jacques disappearing down the stairway. With Frank hot on my heels, I followed him down the stairs, through the lobby and dining room, and then out to the covered porch. Jacques maneuvered around the tables and chairs, down another short staircase to the wide lawn. He curved around, ran about twenty yards more, and stopped, looking up at the main building and panting.

"Look." Frank pointed to the second floor, where we could see the shattered pane. "The break is in the upper left corner of the window. To hit it hard enough to break, the person must have thrown the brick from around where we're standing."

"How do you know that?" Jacques asked, clearly surprised.

"Physics," I replied after a moment. *And way too much experience investigating broken windows.* For now, I figured we'd better keep our sleuthing to ourselves.

Jacques shook his head. "You must like science more than my teenager, Dev."

"Should we call the police?" I asked. Back home in Bayport, the police were sometimes helpful, sometimes not. After some back-and-forth about whether Frank and I were allowed to investigate cases, I'd learned it usually paid off to do things the "right" way, and report crimes that should be reported.

"Rubble Island doesn't have any police," Jacques explained.

"*What?!*" I sputtered. I knew every town was different, but . . . no police at all? In *Maine*? In the twenty-first century?

"Well, technically we're overseen by the force from East Harbor, but nothing really ever happens on the island . . . and the people here prefer to handle petty squabbles among themselves."

"Does a brick through the window count as a 'petty squabble'?" I asked. I was wondering what sort of Wild West ridiculousness Aunt Trudy, Frank, and I had signed up for.

Jacques didn't answer. Instead he held up a hand to get our attention, then very slowly pointed to something on the lawn. I followed his finger. *Footsteps in the grass!* It was a single set—so not left by us—and they led down a short hill to a gate in the fence around the property, one that was still swinging.

"That has to be where the perp went," Frank whispered. "Our brick thrower!"

I didn't need to hear more. Every second counted! I raced down the hill, following the footsteps. I could hear Frank right behind me. The gate exited onto a small path, where old stone steps led to an uneven gravel road. We were behind the inn now, on a road that ran parallel to the water. I could see a few houses along the road ahead, some with lights on inside, but there were no streetlights—no outdoor lights of any kind, really. I wished I had a flashlight.

"Hold on," Frank said, panting as he stopped at my side. "I grabbed my phone on my way out of our room."

Meanwhile, Jacques was calling from the lawn. "Frank! Joe! Come back! It's dark! You'll get lost!"

"We'll be fine," I yelled back.

Frank pulled out his phone from his pj pocket and tapped on the screen to activate the flashlight feature, but it was like a teaspoon's worth of light when we needed about ten gallons.

"Turn it off," I said, looking around. "Remember what they told us in Boy Scouts? Once your eyes adjust, you can get more light from the moon."

Frank flicked off the phone, but my scouting wisdom didn't totally pan out. The moon and the stars *did* look bright up above us—much brighter than at home—but it was still hard to make out anything at ground level against the tall line of dark trees. Still, we followed the gravel road past a few houses. It was impossible to make out footsteps along the well-traveled road, so now we were just guessing about the brick thrower's escape route.

It was eerie; even the houses with lights on were locked up tight. Thick curtains or shutters covered the windows. In the third house down, I could've sworn one window was illuminated, and from a distance we could make out a small living room inside, but when we were a few feet from the path that led to the porch, a hand suddenly snapped the curtains shut.

How do they even know we're here? I wondered. I couldn't help remembering what Colton had said . . . that the islanders didn't care for outsiders.

The gravel road intersected with another at a small building that seemed to be a closed post office. Ahead, the road we were on passed a meadow and led into the dark forest. The other road curved around in the direction of the pier, passing a few more houses and businesses along the way.

A sound like a twig snapping shattered the silence, then something moved through the brush. I looked at Frank.

"This way!" he cried, pointing down the curving road.

I rushed after him, trying to make as little noise as possible, but of course that was hard on a gravel road. After we'd run about thirty yards, Frank held up his hand.

"Do you hear that?" he whispered as he tried to catch his breath.

And then I heard it too: the sound of a body shifting just on the other side of a small storage shed behind the closed ice cream stand. I caught Frank's eye and nodded in the direction of the noise.

Frank's eyes widened. I could feel my body flooding with the adrenaline that always preceded a bad-guy capture. My muscles felt buzzy, and I suddenly felt like I could run for miles. I hoped the perp didn't have a weapon, but even if they did, Frank and I have gotten pretty good at disarming crooks.

Frank held up one finger, *Wait*, and then, after a few seconds, nodded.

Let's go!

We leaped into action, bolting for the shed and splitting up to trap the culprit behind it. As I turned the corner, I saw Frank blinking back at me in confusion. There was no one there. But I was *sure* I'd heard something!

"Rrrrrrroooooowwwww!"

Out of nowhere, a loose collection of paws, teeth, and claws, dark as the night, leaped at me.

"Auuuuuuggghhh!"

I was so stunned I went over like a toy soldier. Before

I knew what was happening, I was sprawled on the damp ground with this *evil force* hissing and scratching at my face.

"*Rrrooow!*"

"It's a cat," Frank said after I'd batted at the demon for a few moments, unsuccessfully trying to dislodge its claws from my face and neck.

"*Oh, is it?*" I could feel blood welling up in the corner of my eye where I'd suffered a particularly nasty scratch. "*Tell me more, Professor!*"

That seemed to shake my brother into action. He pushed at the beast with his foot, which the cat did not like, but at least seemed to respect. Finally, with a last, highly insulted *Mrrrow!*, it jumped off me and disappeared through some low bushes into the night.

Frank's face appeared above mine, looking concerned and, honestly, a little disappointed.

"You could help me up," I snapped as I wiped blood off my cheek.

He held out his hand and I grabbed it, pulling myself to my feet. My whole back was damp with dark, cold mud, from the neck of my T-shirt to the cuffs of my pj pants. I couldn't see what I looked like, but I could feel the scratches and bites crisscrossing my face and chest.

"I guess the island cats don't like outsiders either," Frank said. He was trying to be deadpan, but the corner of his mouth kept twitching.

"Hilarious," I muttered. "Look, I'm guessing we just

scared off our vandal, if they were even out here in the first place."

Frank nodded. "Yeah. Whoever they are, they probably know the island better than we do—which means they know where to hide. The best thing we can do now is go home and clean you up."

We stumbled back to the road, trying to retrace our steps to the inn. When we got to the intersection, I looked both ways, unsettled by the idea that we were surrounded by houses filled with people, and yet not a single soul had come out to see what was going on, even when they must have heard us yelling. In fact, in one house a ways up the road leading into the woods, I could have sworn I saw a face peeking out a window. But just as quickly as I spotted it, it disappeared behind a dark curtain.

What sort of place *was* Rubble Island? Bricks through windows, no cops, evil man-eating cats, and no one to help you when one of those evil cats attacked?

Frank led the way back to the inn. We could see that the lobby was lit, and that figures were sitting around a long wooden table inside. When we stepped onto the porch, all eyes turned toward us, and Aunt Trudy stood and let out a cry of relief.

"Boys, you're okay! Oh—what happened to you, Joe?"

I pushed open the door. "A monster masquerading as a cat," I explained. "Bad timing on our part. We didn't find whoever threw the brick."

Aunt Trudy clucked in sympathy while Jacques jumped up. "Let me get some bandages, and a cloth to clean you up. Have a seat." He disappeared down a hallway that I assumed led to his living quarters.

Colton and Gemma were already sitting at the table. Colton hugged a cup of what smelled like chamomile tea. "It was brave of you boys to go after the guy," he said, looking up.

Frank shrugged. "It was no big deal. It's kind of what we do." Then he frowned. "Is there a reason you think it's a guy?"

Colton looked startled, but he glanced down into his mug again and shook his head. "No, no. I have no idea who it was. I suppose I'm being sexist."

Gemma chuckled. "Yes, Colton. Petty vandals can be women, too."

Jacques came back with a box of Band-Aids, a damp washcloth, and a small bottle of hydrogen peroxide. He took the seat next to mine and motioned me to face him. "This will sting," he said, washing my face and neck with the cloth and then putting some hydrogen peroxide on it and gently patting the wounds. For a little while, I concentrated on not yelping at the burning sensation as the hydrogen peroxide touched each scratch and bite.

"Is there a lot of vandalism on the island?" Frank asked. "I mean, is it unusual for you to have a brick thrown at the inn?"

Jacques was focused on cleaning my wounds, so he didn't look up. "It's a small island. You know what they say about familiarity breeding contempt. People have their differences. Things happen. But it doesn't usually lead to violence."

"On such a small island, doesn't it make sense to be *more* careful how you treat your neighbors?" I asked. "You know, you throw a brick through someone's window, then you run into them at the coffee shop. *Awkward!*"

Jacques laughed. "Well, the inn is different. Islanders are private. They don't care much for outsiders. *I* wasn't terribly popular when I bought the Sea Spray ten years ago. They saw me as this snooty French Canadian, taking over a piece of their beloved island history. It took me a long time to earn people's trust."

"But you have?" Frank said. "Earned their trust, I mean?"

Jacques sighed. Suddenly he looked very tired. I remembered it was the middle of the night after a long day for us all. "Look," he said. "To be honest? The person who threw the brick was probably someone upset that Colton was coming and bringing a bunch of city people with him. The islanders just don't want any trouble. They like their quiet life."

Frank shook his head. "That's a crummy reason to throw a brick at someone."

For a few seconds, an awkward silence descended over the group.

Colton ended it. Taking a last swig of his tea, he stood up and turned toward the stairs. "Listen, we shouldn't make too much of this. . . . It was probably just someone trying to scare me. Anyway, I'm exhausted, and we should all get to bed. I'm heading up to my new room. There's a rooster on the island, and he'll be waking everyone up in about six hours." After Colton had gone, it wasn't long before the rest of us followed.

Aunt Trudy and Gemma passed us as they went down the hallway to their rooms. Colton was fumbling with the lock on the door next to ours while Frank dug in his pocket for our key. I was just standing there, idly watching them both.

Before Colton could disappear inside his new room, I leaned in close and touched his shoulder. "Are you sure you're okay, man? That must have been really scary."

Colton's jaw tightened. "I'm fine," he said stiffly. "Thank you for asking. Good night." He pulled away, walked through the door, and shut it quickly—barely leaving me time to pull my hand back.

Frank had gotten our door open. He raised an eyebrow at me, and then we both went inside. "What was that?"

"I noticed something, and I wanted to take a closer look to confirm it," I whispered back. "Colton's robe pocket had a folded-up note written in thick black marker. You know what that means?"

Frank's eyes lit up. "I'm guessing the vandal wrapped a note around the brick . . . and it's something Colton doesn't want us to see."

MEET CUTE 5

FRANK

COLTON HADN'T BEEN KIDDING ABOUT that rooster—he was up at six and had some lungs on him.

Rustled from our beds, Joe and I chatted about what'd happened the night before. "Why would Colton hide the note?" I asked. "Especially since whoever sent it was targeting him."

Joe shook his head as he dug around in his suitcase. "All I can think is there's something in that note he doesn't want us to know," he replied.

I sighed. "Wow." This trip was supposed to be time to relax and watch Aunt Trudy live out her dream. "Rubble Island seems like a lot more than I was bargaining for."

Joe pulled on a T-shirt. "More like *Trouble* Island, amirite?"

I groaned. "Please never say that again."

"Anyway, it definitely seems like something weird is happening here."

"Right," I said. "Everyone keeps talking about the islanders not liking outsiders . . . but it really seems like Colton is less welcome than anyone else would be."

"Remember what happened in East Harbor?"

I grunted. The image of the guy from the general store spitting in our direction wasn't one I'd forget soon. Clearly, Colton was unpopular in this part of Maine, but why? What was he hiding?

By the time we went downstairs for breakfast, around eight o'clock, Aunt Trudy had already eaten and was working on food prep with Colton in the kitchen. It looked like a couple of the "local helpers" had shown up. Colton, wearing an orange polo shirt with a tiny chili pepper embroidered on it, had two people over on the far side of the kitchen chopping vegetables, occasionally berating them about their knife skills being garbage: "You hold it at a *forty-five-degree* angle! Honestly, who trained you?!"

The helpers glanced at each other, shrugged, and corrected their knife angles. Colton rolled his eyes and stared out the window. I was glad Aunt Trudy didn't seem to be a target too.

"Are you boys hungry?" she asked. "Oh, Joe. Your poor face! Does it hurt?"

"Only when I move," Joe replied.

Aunt Trudy sighed. "Oof. Well, Polly left us some

delicious scones with clotted cream, fruit salad, hard-boiled eggs. . . ." She indicated the walk-in pantry, and the industrial-size refrigerator beside it. There was enough food in the pantry to feed a small army. Huge sacks of organic sweet potatoes and onions lined the floor. We grabbed scones from a container on the counter, then turned our attention to the refrigerator. The shelves were stacked with different kinds of fancy cheeses, produce, meats, and other goodies. We each grabbed what we wanted, then walked back out into the kitchen, where Aunt Trudy pointed us toward the coffee and tea.

"Are you ready?" I asked with a smile. "Only one day to go." Colton was still on the other side of the kitchen, muttering under his breath as he stirred a huge vat of what looked like broth.

Aunt Trudy nodded, but I could see from the tension in her face that she was feeling a little harried. She leaned in close. "Only two of the five promised 'helpers' from the mainland arrived on the ferry this morning," she whispered.

"Two of five? Do you know why?"

Aunt Trudy shrugged. "All Colton will say is that it's so hard to find reliable help. Who would turn down the opportunity to learn from a celebrity chef?"

"Even if the locals don't like outsiders, surely there are *some* foodies around here?" Joe said.

Aunt Trudy glanced nervously over her shoulder. "I suggested finding some islanders who might help, but Colton changed the subject."

At that moment, the chef in question looked up. "Trudy! Would you mind working with Celine and Tom for a few minutes? Maybe you can teach them proper knife skills, since they clearly aren't listening to me!"

"Of course," Aunt Trudy called back, before heading across the kitchen. Honestly, Colton seemed like a bit of a prima donna to me, but I was glad to see that Aunt Trudy seemed to jibe with him in a weird way. The two helpers looked relieved when she demonstrated chopping an onion, talking to them quietly and calmly. Colton also seemed relieved and went back to his broth.

Joe and I waved at Aunt Trudy before carrying our breakfast into the empty dining room.

"We need to figure out what's going on," I said, spreading jam on my (delicious) scone. "This is Aunt Trudy's big chance to live out her dream. I don't want her to lose out on that, and I definitely don't want to see her put in any danger."

"Agreed," Joe said. "We've got to get to the bottom of this for Aunt Trudy."

"Then I guess it's time for us to meet some islanders and learn more about Rubble Island."

Joe's eyes widened. "You mean *Trouble*—"

"Please stop. Let's not make that a thing."

"Jacques has some trail maps down in the lobby," I said as Joe and I headed upstairs. "We should grab some. Maybe if we get the lay of the land today in daylight, we'll be ready if something else happens tonight."

Joe nodded. "Some of the trails are marked 'difficult,'" he said. "If we do those, let's make time for a nap later."

"Aw, come on."

Joe scowled. "Frank, we're supposed to be on vacation."

I paused outside the room next to ours. "Seriously, if you're this lazy now, what are you going to be like when you're middle-aged?"

"Like myself, but better." He pulled out a multi-tool from his wallet. "Like a Joe that's had more practice." He knelt down and peered at the lock, then carefully inserted the flat screwdriver blade between the door and the frame, sliding it up, then down, then to the right. Finally there was a *click* and the door popped open.

We glanced around the hallway, then slipped into Colton Sparks's room.

The space was tidy and unremarkable. It hadn't been made up yet, but Colton's things were stacked neatly in his suitcase, and through the open bathroom door, we could see his toiletries arranged in a small bag. We'd been looking around a little bit, careful not to make too much noise, when Joe nudged me and pointed. Colton's bathrobe was hanging on the bathroom door. *Jackpot!*

While I played lookout, Joe carefully reached into the robe's pocket. He slowly pulled out the note, unfolded it, and aimed it in my direction. As we'd planned, I pulled my phone out of my pocket and was just snapping a picture when we heard the unmistakable sound of a housekeeping cart being pushed up the hall.

I caught Joe's eye. *Yikes!* We hadn't really had time to work out an escape route from Colton's room if someone was blocking the door, and seeing as the building dated back to the early twentieth century, it seemed safe to assume there weren't a lot of emergency exits. Quickly Joe put the folded paper back in Colton's robe pocket. We'd have time to examine the photo on my phone later.

"So I told her, listen, there's no way I'm doing all *your* errands. . . ." The housekeeper seemed to be talking on her phone as she made her way down the hallway. I remembered with a groan that Colton's room, now that he'd moved, was the first in the line of those occupied by the Golden Claw Awards party. It only made sense that the housekeeper would start here, which meant we had no time to sneak out into the hall and past the housekeeper without being seen.

"What do we do?" I whispered to Joe as we heard the cart park just outside the door.

He shrugged, his eyes darting around the room. "We could hide under the bed? Or in the closet?"

I shook my head. "Are you new? She's the *housekeeper*, Joe. She'll be cleaning those places."

Joe looked a little hurt. "Only if she's a *good* housekeeper."

"Let's assume she is."

I could hear the key being inserted in the lock. We had

only seconds to get out of sight. I nudged Joe hard with my elbow and pointed to the large bay window. Thank goodness the side windows opened out and there were no screens, so we could scramble onto the sloping roof. The door opened as we scooched down the weathered wooden shingles, just out of sight.

Holding our breath, we waited a few moments. When we didn't hear a cry of alarm, I knew we were safe—for now. Wordlessly, Joe pointed out toward the water. Rubble Island's harbor was even more stunningly beautiful than it had been when we'd sailed in the previous afternoon. And since we were so high up, we could see the ocean spreading out between Seal and Heron Rocks all the way to the mainland. The rocky coast of the island curved around toward the woods to our left, and the tiny village stretched to our right.

"Gorgeous," I said softly.

Joe pointed at the harbor. "Look. I think that guy sees us." There was a man in canvas overalls and black rubber boots moving some lobster traps from the pier onto his boat. Cautiously, I raised my hand in greeting, and sure enough, he waved back. He was wearing a hat with a green-and-black-stripe pattern on the front.

We heard a loud *click* behind us farther up the roof. I glanced back just in time to see the housekeeper, a young woman with her dark hair in a ponytail, stepping away from the window—which she'd clearly just locked.

"Great," Joe muttered, following my eye to the window. "Well, I guess it's time we figured out how to get down from here."

We were too high to jump, but there didn't seem to be any easy path down. We crawled around the roof, trying not to attract attention, before I spotted our best bet: the covered porch facing the harbor, where most of the guests ate breakfast. It was late in the morning. We *probably* could sneak by undetected.

"We just have to time it right," Joe said after I explained my plan.

"Right," I agreed.

Slowly, and as silently as we could, we made our way over to the corner of the roof. The only noise we could hear was the calling of seagulls as they swooped around overhead. The lawn, the porch, the whole inn seemed to be under a silent spell.

We scooted out over the covered porch and dangled our legs over the edge by a post that led to a waist-high railing. Joe went first, carefully wrapping his legs around the post and shinnying down. He stood on the railing, then jumped off onto the lawn. It was a good jump—six feet or so—but he landed easily, then turned around, grinning up at me.

"Piece of cake," he called. "Come on, Frank. Let's get out of here."

I followed his lead. When my feet hit the railing, I stood up, then swung my right foot off and jumped down onto the lawn.

I missed slightly, landing partly in a scraggly, just-budding bush. Still, apart from a few scratches, I was intact, and considering where we'd started, that felt like a victory.

"All right!" I cried, getting to my feet. "Hardy Boys one, Sea Spray Inn zero! Amirite?"

Then I noticed the look on Joe's face. He did not look like I was "rite." He glanced at me quickly, then back at the porch, pointing awkwardly into the shadows.

Huddled under one of the porch's eaves, in a corner near a potted plant, stood a boy slightly younger than Joe. He had in wireless earbuds and was clearly listening to something on his phone.

"Hi," he said, unhooking one earbud and looking right at us.

LAY OF THE LAND

6

JOE

I," I REPLIED. I CONSIDER MYSELF pretty smooth—I mean, definitely compared to Frank—but even I was struggling to keep it cool and breezy. This dude had just watched us casually climb off the hotel's roof. What possible explanation could there be for that?

He moved closer to us, pointing up at the porch overhang. "Were you guys checking out the widow's walk?"

"Ah," said Frank, looking up at the roof and gesturing like some disco robot. See, it's not hard to seem smooth compared to him.

"It's supercool," the boy said. As he stepped into a beam of sunlight, I could see that he had a medium-brown complexion, with chocolate eyes and wavy, chin-length chestnut hair. "My dad decided it was too dangerous to let guests go up there because the steps are kind of steep and the railing is old and not really high enough for kids. Last year he closed off the stairway on the inside of the building. Now you can only get there from the roof. You're not *really* supposed to go up there, but I love to, honestly. You can't beat the view. Don't worry, I won't tell."

"Thanks," I said with a smile. "Yeah, it's amazing up there. I'm sorry, you said your dad closed it off?"

"Yeah," the boy said, holding out his hand. "I should introduce myself. I'm Dev, Jacques's son. I was working with a friend on a school project last night, so I missed dinner."

Ahhh. The son Jacques had mentioned last night. I shook his hand. "Nice to meet you. I'm Joe Hardy, and this is my older brother, Frank."

Dev smiled and shook Frank's hand too. Then he reached up to pull out his other earbud before sticking them in his pocket. "Are you guys with Colton Sparks's group?"

"That's right," Frank said. "But we're not really *part* of the group. We're just kind of . . . group-adjacent."

When Dev looked confused, I explained, "We're here with our aunt, who won the chance to be Colton's intern. Our school's on vacation this week, and Aunt Trudy was allowed to bring guests, so we decided to tag along."

"Cool," said Dev, nodding. "Your aunt must be a great cook."

"The best," I agreed. "And she's a big fan of Colton's, so

this is a lot of fun for her. Do you go to the school here on the island?"

"Yeah." Dev glanced at his watch. "It's tiny. There are, like, fifteen of us for all of kindergarten through twelfth."

"That must be interesting," Frank said.

Dev ran a hand through his hair, pinning it behind one ear. "*Interesting*, yeah. It's actually kind of cool. You really get to know your classmates, and the older kids help teach the younger ones. I'm in tenth grade."

"Are you on vacation this week too?" I asked.

"Actually, no." Dev shook his head. "We don't get a break until Easter. But today is the start of lobster season, which is kind of a big deal, so we have it off."

"The start of lobster season?" Frank asked. "I thought you could lobster year-round. At least, that's what I saw online when I was getting ready for our trip."

"You *can*," Dev explained, "but a few years ago, the lobstermen and -women on Rubble Island got together and mutually agreed to take the winters off so that the lobster population could grow back up, and they could take advantage of the higher summer prices. Lobstering can be a competitive, nasty business—a guy a few islands away got shot a several years back for trapping on another lobsterman's territory. Folks here want to avoid all that, so they try to work together."

"That's cool," I said. "What happens on the first day of the season that makes it so special?"

Dev smiled and shrugged. "Come with me to the pier and see for yourself. I was just about to head down there."

I looked at Frank. I hadn't forgotten about the note from Colton's room, but this seemed like too good an opportunity to pass up. After all, if we were looking to learn more about Rubble Island, I couldn't think of a better way to do that than to go exploring with a local. Frank nodded, and I could tell from his expression that he was thinking the same thing I was.

"That sounds great," he said. "Lead the way!"

Dev strolled across the lawn, taking the path we'd followed the previous afternoon, down the gravel road toward the pier. As we got closer, we saw a bunch of people gathered—maybe a hundred or more—and they all seemed very interested in us.

"Who's that you got witcha, Dev?" a white-haired man in a baseball hat that read ALDEMERE FARM asked as we wove through the crowd.

"Just some guests from the inn, Bill," Dev called back with a smile.

"Colton Sparks's guests?" a woman with curly red hair asked, but Dev pretended not to hear. *They all know Colton Sparks is here with guests?* Just how quickly did word travel on this island?

When we got to the front, Dev waved at a girl about our age who had her long blond hair in a ponytail under a Red Sox cap. She waved back, then returned her attention to a group of men and women in work gear—lobster people.

Frank tugged on my sleeve. "First opportunity we get, we need to look at that note," he whispered into my ear.

I nodded. "Yeah. But we need a second away from Dev."

Just then a voice announced, "Welcome to opening day for Rubble Island's lobstering season!" A gray-haired man with a curly beard was speaking into a megaphone.

Everyone cheered.

"I'm Bruce Fenton, and as most of you know, Rubble Island decided a few years back to limit our lobstering to the warmer seasons. This makes us unique among Maine's lobstering communities and is just one more thing that shows what a special island this is."

"Let's keep it that way!" a female voice screeched from the back of the crowd, and a bunch of voices shouted their support. The audience began applauding loudly.

When the noise died down, Bruce called, "We agree on that. We all need to do everything we can to protect our way of life here."

I caught Frank's eye. I was thinking about what Colton had said the day before—how the islanders wanted to keep Rubble Island for themselves and didn't like outsiders. This sounded different, like the islanders felt they were somehow under threat.

"Anyway," Bruce went on, "I think we're mostly locals here, and I know none of you like to hear me yammer on. Let's get to the good stuff, shall we? Who's ready to get this year's lobstering season started?!"

"We're ready!" a twentysomething guy with a blond goatee yelled back.

On the pier, the lobster people took their places.

Bruce raised the megaphone to his lips, paused for dramatic effect, then yelled, "Let's go!"

At least ten different lobstering crews jumped into action, among them Dev's friend, moving large wire lobster traps onto a collection of lobster boats tied up at the docks.

"What are they doing?" I asked Dev. "What's the rush?"

"Oh, they'll all place their traps on the ocean floor today," Dev explained. "It's kind of first come, first serve, so everyone jostles to get the best spots. Each crew ends up with his or her own territory, and they use colorful buoys to tell them apart. See those patterns? Those are the crews' insignias. Each boat or company has its own."

We watched the action for a few minutes. The lobster people were clearly focused, but everyone seemed to be in a good mood, smiling and laughing with one another, even if they bumped into one another or had to pass each other on the dock.

"Does anyone ever pull up another boat's traps and steal their lobsters?" I whispered to Dev.

He turned, his eyes wide. "Not if they want to live. This is a small island. Everyone knows where to find you."

After we watched for another twenty minutes, the crowd started to disperse. Dev's friend waved at him as she got on a boat with an older woman. Dev waved back and called out, "Good luck!"

"Who's that?" Frank asked.

"My friend Trish. That boat's been in her family for three generations. Her grandmother was the first lobsterwoman to own her own boat on Rubble Island. Now there are a bunch of female-led crews. Pretty cool, huh?"

"Very cool," I agreed. "It looks like hard work, though."

"Definitely," Dev said. "But they love it. Hey, you guys want coffee?"

I looked around. "Back at the inn, you mean?"

Dev shook his head. "No need to go back there. Jerry at the Gull makes the best cappuccino I've ever had. You in?"

"Sure," Frank said. "Sounds good to me!" He shot me a look that said, *Probably lots of islanders at the Gull.*

I nodded.

When Dev pulled ahead of us, Frank moved to my side. "Quick look at the note?" he whispered.

"Good call," I whispered back, pulling out my phone. But no sooner had I brought up the photo than Dev waved.

"Hurry up, guys!" he yelled. "We have to beat the crowds!"

Sure enough, as soon as I turned around, I saw half the spectators from the season opening headed in the same direction. Assuming there was only one barista, there'd be a long wait if we didn't hustle.

"Shoot," Joe muttered, putting his phone back in his pocket.

I shrugged. "Yeah, but if the whole town's headed to the same place, maybe we'll get some intel on who's got it out for Colton, and why."

"Let's keep our ears open and see what we can find out," Joe suggested.

We followed Dev to a small red cottage just off the pier with a hand-painted sign out front: THE GULL COFFEE SHOP AND GENERAL STORE.

But as Dev pushed open the screen door, the place went silent. It was beginning to make me kind of paranoid, this ability we seemed to have to stop conversations all over Maine dead in their tracks.

Dev cleared his throat. "Hey, everyone. I want to introduce you to my friends, Joe and Frank Hardy. They're staying at the Sea Spray because their aunt won a contest."

"So they're not part of Colton Sparks's entourage?" a man sitting at the counter asked. I realized it was the same guy who I'd seen on the pier wearing the ALDEMERE FARM hat—Bill. There was no disguising the scorn in his voice.

"We're not," I said. "I mean, we're traveling with him, but we don't know him that well."

We heard murmurs and mutters as the Gull customers discussed this new nugget with their neighbors.

Finally the woman behind the counter spoke up. "Well, welcome to Rubble Island, Joe and Frank Hardy," she said warmly. "Can I getcha somethin' to drink?"

Dev led us over and introduced the woman as Jerry McNath, lifelong Rubble Island resident and the owner of the Gull. We ordered our cappuccinos, and Jerry got to work making the espresso and steaming the milk. Around us, the other customers seemed to fold back into their separate conversations.

As Frank and I watched Jerry work, I decided it was time to be direct. And anyway, the curiosity was killing me. Leaning over the counter, I let out a nervous laugh. "So what is it that Rubble Island has against Colton Sparks?"

Jerry kept her focus on frothing, but I could tell she'd heard me. "Do you boys know anything about the history of the island?" she asked.

"A little," Frank said.

"Well, let me fill you in." Jerry pulled out three bowl-like mugs. "Rubble Island is older than the United States. It was discovered by Native Americans, probably back in the sixteenth century. Before Europeans ever settled on the mainland of North America, Rubble Island was used as a fishing outpost for both Native Americans and Europeans. That's right—the Norwegians and the English used to send boats out every summer to fish our waters. They got a taste for American seafood long before any white person thought about settling here."

That surprised me. "Did the Native Americans live here, then?"

"No, they never settled here full-time. Too remote, I think. But they would make fishing trips and camp for a few days. They've found a bunch of Native American artifacts up on Lighthouse Hill—that's where researchers think they might've stayed."

Jerry poured a shot of espresso into each cup, then picked up her metal pitcher, poured in generous dollops of foam, and pushed the cups across the counter.

"Hope you like 'em bone dry. That's the only way I make 'em. And I don't do any fancy pictures. You want that, go to Portland or something."

She said *Portland* with the kind of scorn most New Englanders seemed to reserve for Yankees fans.

"So who *did* settle here first?" Frank asked.

Jerry smiled. "Funny you should ask. In the 1800s, Rubble Island became one of the first artist colonies in the United States. It was only active in the summer, but it housed some very influential artists of the day. In the 1930s, we became a federally recognized wildlife preserve. There are species of birds here that aren't found anywhere else in the continental US. And of course . . . well, since the 1920s or so, we've been a working fishing and lobstering island."

"Only since then?" I asked.

Jerry nodded. "Fun fact, boys: lobster has only been considered a luxury food since World War II. Before that, they used to feed it to prisoners, and back in colonial days it was goat food. Have you ever looked at a lobster? It looks like a giant bug or an alien. You have to wonder, who was the first guy to think about eating *that*? But then the marketing suits got hold of them, and *whoo!* Now nobody can get enough of 'em."

I took a sip of my cappuccino. *Dang.* It was perfect.

"Anyway," Jerry went on, "my point is, Rubble Island has

a long history and plenty to recommend it all on its own. We don't need Colton Sparks to 'discover' our island and bring all his fancy chef folks out here. We don't want to be 'discovered.' We want to be left alone. I prefer Polly's food to anything Colton Sparks dishes up, anyway."

I could tell Frank was about to ask something, but Dev spoke first. "How much time do you guys have today? I could show you around some more."

Frank shrugged. "Kind of . . . all day?" he said, at exactly the same time I coughed and said, "Well, we really should get back to the inn."

In the awkward moment that followed, Frank and I stared at each other. I tried to subtly point at Frank's jeans pocket, the one I knew held his phone. *We have to read that note!*

Dev looked from me to Frank. "It would be a shame if you came all this way and just saw the village and the inn. I could take you on a tour of the hiking trails that wind through the preserve, show you sights the tourists don't even know about!"

Frank looked at me. "That sounds gre—"

"I need to use the restroom," I said loudly, cutting Frank off. Maybe a little *too* loudly, judging from the expressions on the faces of the other customers around us. I didn't care— as long as Frank got the message.

"Uh," he finally said. "Yeah, that's a good idea. I need to go too. Coffee, you know! Ha!"

Jerry frowned. "The bathroom here isn't exactly public, but I'll let you use it if you're dyin'."

I nodded. "I'm dyin'. Thank you!"

"Yeah, definitely!" Frank echoed.

Jerry gestured to a black-painted door behind the counter. "Come on back here, then. Knock yourselves out."

Dev smiled. "I'll wait for you guys," he said, lifting his phone. "Trish says they have almost all the traps placed. Maybe she can meet up with us later."

"Her phone works on the lobster boat?" Frank asked, sounding impressed.

"Oh yeah. A few years ago, they built a cell tower out here—entering the twenty-first century and all that—but I think it works best with local carriers."

Truth. I'd had on-and-off service since we'd arrived.

"You go first," I said, gesturing to the bathroom and widening my eyes at Frank.

He nodded and touched the pocket of his jeans. "Right."

In our developed-over-time Hardy brothers secret language, this meant, *I get it. I'll read the note on my phone, then pass it on to you. Let's do this.*

After a short wait, Frank came out with a wide-eyed look. He held out his phone, shoving it into my hands.

"Hey, Joe," he said, all faux casually. "You have to check out this *supercute puppy video* I just watched. I bookmarked it for you."

"Thanks," I said, grabbing the phone eagerly and swerving around him into the bathroom.

I was so excited to read the note that I forgot that

bathrooms have doors and light switches. At the last minute, I remembered to close the door behind me, which plunged me into pitch darkness. I didn't want to open the door again and draw attention to my foolishness, so I felt around the wall on either side of the door, searching for a switch, but when I finally found it, I was so excited that I fumbled the phone out of my hands.

"*No!*" I watched it drop into the toilet in slow motion, remembering a second later to dive for it, and by some miracle, grabbed it with both hands just before it hit the water.

"*Yes!*"

But my relief was short-lived. No sooner had I lifted the phone out of the bowl than I heard that unmistakable *bloop* delete sound.

Turning the screen to face me, I desperately hoped I could still save the image, but as my finger furiously mashed at the icon, I heard the dreaded *whoosh*. I'd deleted the photo of the note—*forever*. I sat down on the toilet, doing everything I could think of to get the photo back, even googling *Get photo back deleted accidentally why help!!*

It didn't turn up any useful results.

Someone knocked on the door.

"Are you still in there, Joe?" Frank called. "Everything *okay?*"

"It's fine! I'm fine!" I yelled, standing up and flushing the toilet for appearances. *Frank read the note*, I reminded myself. *Frank can tell me what it said. . . .*

I opened the door to find Frank, Dev, and half of Rubble Island watching me curiously.

"You ready?" Dev asked, looking slightly concerned. "I bought us some water and snacks. Are you allergic to nuts?"

I wondered how long I'd been in there, exactly.

"No, nuts are great," I replied, waving at Jerry, who nodded with an amused smirk. "As am I. I feel great." But when Dev turned and began leading us back outside, I shoved the phone into Frank's hand. "I deleted it," I said though gritted teeth.

"You *deleted* it?" he whispered back. "Seriously?"

"I didn't *mean* to. I just—"

"Are you guys sure you're up for a hike?" Dev called back. He had walked farther onto the pier, and I realized that Frank and I had fallen really far behind. Worse, we must've looked pretty rude, whispering away while he was standing right there.

"We're sure," I said, shooting Frank a look that said, *later.* "Sorry. We were just catching up on back-home gossip. We can't wait to see more of Rubble Island."

Dev smiled. "Great. Because I can't wait to show it to you."

SOMETHING'S OFF

7

FRANK

"THAT WAS AMAZING," I SAID AS WE stepped from the gravel road onto the Sea Spray Inn's lawn later that afternoon. "But I'm going to be sore tomorrow!"

Dev laughed. "Sorry, guys. I hope I didn't overdo it. There's just so much to see! I think the island's really one of the most beautiful places I've ever been. Unfortunately, a lot of the prettiest stuff is up a steep slope or through spiky brush."

"Don't worry about it," Joe said, clapping Dev on the back. "You can't find the sights you showed us today on a postcard. I had no idea Rubble Island had so much to see."

So much was right. We'd spent hours wandering through the woods and along the rocky cliffs that led down to the sea. Dev had shown us a whirlpool where the tides formed a tiny tornado in the sea, and the remains of a shipwreck from the early 1900s. We'd also seen more wildlife than I had ever seen in one place before. It was clear why the nature preserve was so needed.

By the time we got back, it was nearing dusk. Lanterns on the porch cast slanted golden light over the lawn, which was beginning to take on an inky darkness. We'd seen the beginning of a spectacular sunset over the water on the far side of the island just before we turned back.

"Looks like clouds are moving in," Dev said, pointing to the sky above the harbor. Now that he mentioned it, the wind was picking up. "I hope that doesn't cause trouble for Colton and his awards tomorrow."

"Why would it?" Joe asked.

"Living on an island ten miles out to sea, you learn to pay close attention to the weather," Dev explained. "When a storm rolls in, the ferry can't get out here, and neither can the mail, groceries . . ."

". . . or all the fancy chefs coming in for the awards," I finished.

Dev nodded. "I hope for Colton's sake it blows through. I know he's got a lot riding on these awards."

A lot riding on these awards? I wondered what Dev meant by that. Before I could ask, he climbed the porch steps and went inside. Colton was an already famous TV chef with restaurants all over the country. What could he have riding on a small awards banquet? I wondered if it had something to do with the note in his robe.

As Joe and I walked into the lobby, we were greeted by a warm, comforting smell: garlic, butter, seafood, tomatoes. *Mmm.* I'd forgotten that one of the benefits of traveling with a celebrity chef was that said celebrity chef cooked *you* dinner.

"Aunt Trudy?" Joe called. "Colton? We're back!"

She suddenly popped through the dining room door, wearing a big smile. "Oh, hello! I'm Trudy. I don't think we've met before," she said, holding out her hand to Dev.

"It's very nice to meet you," he said, nodding politely. "I've been showing your nephews around the island. Have you been having fun with Colton?"

Aunt Trudy let out a squeal of delight. "Have I! Oh, you've all arrived just in time! The fish is perfect, if I say so myself. Did you get to see the whole island, boys?"

I nodded. "Dev gave us the grand tour. It's really amazing, Aunt Trudy. If you can get out of the kitchen, even for an hour, you have to take a look around."

She smiled. "Maybe after the awards I'll get up early and do just that." She turned to Dev. "Have you all worked up an appetite?"

Dev held up a hand. "Thanks, Trudy, but I'm actually going to grab a soda in the kitchen and then excuse myself. I'm working on an independent project for school that's due tomorrow and I still have some writing to finish."

Aunt Trudy raised her eyebrows. "Oh! What are you studying?"

Dev chuckled. "It's food science, actually. Ironic, right?"

Aunt Trudy laughed. "Maybe you can teach me a thing or two, along with Colton. Let me make you a plate to bring upstairs."

"That would be great. Thank you."

As Aunt Trudy retreated back into the kitchen, I turned to Dev. "Sorry, man. I hope we didn't keep you away from your project all day."

"Oh, no worries. I would *always* rather be outside than cooped up working, and today was a beautiful day to hike. It was my choice to show you guys around, and I don't regret it. I just need to get down to work now." He nodded at us and headed into the kitchen.

A few minutes later, Aunt Trudy came out and waved us into the dining room. "Come on. Sit down. I'm going to go find Gemma and Jacques, but the salad's already out. Help yourselves to that and some freshly baked bread."

"Sounds great." We settled down at the table and tore off some still-warm bread. (*Yum!*)

"So?" Joe asked eagerly. "What did the note say?"

"I don't remember the exact words," I whispered, "but something like, Colton's not welcome here, and he'd better watch his step—accidents happen on the island all the time, and sometimes they're not even accidents."

Joe's eyes widened. "'Not even accidents'? That sounds like a threat!"

"Yeah. And not a subtle one."

"What would a small island in Maine have against a celebrity chef? I know Jerry said they don't need him here, but ..."

"But it has to be more than that," I said. "There's something Colton isn't telling us—and I bet it has to do with how sudden this whole trip was."

Just then Aunt Trudy came back into the dining room, looking tired but happy. "Gemma's on her way down. How's the bread?"

"It's delicious," Joe said before stuffing another piece in his mouth.

"Well, Colton showed me how to use steam in the oven to get a nice, shiny crust. Really, he's teaching me so much every minute! By the time we're finished with this banquet, I'll be ready to open my own restaurant."

"Do you want to do that?" asked Joe.

Aunt Trudy laughed. "Not really. But it's nice to think I could."

I grinned. "Hey, listen, Aunt Trudy—while you were working with Colton today, did he say anything else about the islanders not liking him?"

She looked thoughtful, then shook her head. "Well, there was . . . It was about the brick, not about the islanders. He thinks it was just a random act of vandalism."

"That may be true," Joe said, frowning, "but the thing is—"

"The thing is, the island is really beautiful!" I said quickly. Joe glanced at me, surprised, but I plowed ahead. "I could see why they'd want to keep it for themselves. It's not like any place I've ever seen before."

Aunt Trudy nodded happily. When she excused herself to go back to the kitchen, Joe shot me another quizzical look.

"She's having the time of her life," I whispered. "Let's not ruin it for her before we even know what's going on."

A few minutes later Gemma and Jacques joined us at the table, and then Colton and Aunt Trudy came out, carrying serving dish after dish. There were roasted tomatoes with goat cheese, Mediterranean couscous, and the pièce de résistance—haddock roasted with garlic and olives, served in a butter-wine sauce.

"This looks delicious!" Jacques exclaimed, rubbing his hands together.

"Yeah, you guys really knocked yourselves out," Gemma added. "It makes me feel guilty that I was just reading in my room all day."

"You didn't explore at all?" I asked her, surprised.

Gemma shook her head as she unfolded her napkin and placed it in her lap. "Maybe tomorrow. We've been traveling so much. I needed a 'relax' day."

"Tomorrow might not work out," Jacques said as we began to serve ourselves. "A storm is blowing in. I hope it won't affect your guests' passage tomorrow, Colton."

"So do I," Colton agreed. "According to my phone, the storm should rage all night but clear up in the morning. It may be perfect timing."

"That's good news," Jacques replied. "Let's hope the report's accurate."

As we passed the food around, we could hear the wind pick up outside, howling around the sides of the building and flapping the decorative SEA SPRAY INN flag out in the yard.

"Should we be worried?" Gemma asked, looking from the windows to Jacques. "That wind sounds pretty serious."

"Not at all. We feel storms strongly out here in the middle of the ocean, but the inn has been standing for over one hundred years. We'll be fine."

Feeling reassured, we dug into our meal. I'm not the biggest fish fan—at least fish that *looks* like fish, which this totally did—but there was so much food, I was able to push it to the side and chow down on my side dishes, which tasted pretty amazing. We chatted amiably about the plans for the Golden Claw Awards, how the dining room would be set up, when the film crew would arrive—because Colton wanted to show excerpts on some of his shows. "Everyone needs to know about this island!" he said. "It's something special I want to share with my viewers."

I caught Joe's eye and could tell he was thinking the same thing I was: *But do the islanders want their home shared?*

"We went to watch the ceremony for lobster season opening day," Joe said casually.

"Oh, that's right. That was today," Jacques replied. "I usually go, but I was fixing the broken window."

I felt a flood of gratitude that Joe and I hadn't ended up on the roof at the exact moment Jacques went up to do his repairs.

"It's really cool how the lobstermen and -women banded together to create this season," I said. "It seems like they work really hard. They probably need the time off."

Jacques nodded. "Everyone needs a work-life balance! It's like—"

Colton pushed his chair back with a screech, clamping his hand over his mouth. He was bright red.

"Colton!" Gemma cried. "Are you—?"

He leaped up from the table and raced to the small bathroom off the dining room, slamming the door behind him. In the silence that followed, we could hear him retching.

"Well," Joe said. "Um, did Colton—?"

He was cut off by the screech of another chair. Aunt Trudy was looking kind of pink too. "How strange," she said. "I suddenly—I don't feel great." She stood shakily, then ran out to the lobby and up the staircase. We could hear her speeding along the hallway and fumbling with the lock on her room's door.

Gemma looked around at the remaining faces. "Uh. Okay. Is everybody—"

Joe groaned. A few seconds later, he was bolting for our room. And Jacques looked a little peaked too, though he seemed to be holding it together better than the others. When the door to the ground-floor bathroom slammed open and Colton staggered out, Gemma jumped up to run in there herself. A minute or so later, Aunt Trudy stumbled back to rejoin the group, but she didn't look much better.

"What's happening?" I asked. I still felt okay—although watching everyone at the table looking queasy was making me wonder.

Colton groaned. "Isn't it obvious? Food poisoning!"

"You think?" I asked as Joe slowly dragged himself into the room.

"It's the only explanation," Jacques said, still clearly struggling to keep his food down. "We were all fine until we ate. What do we think it could have been?"

Colton moaned again. "Everything was cooked properly. It doesn't make sense. . . ."

"I think it's the fish," I said. "I feel okay, and I didn't eat that much of it." I shot an apologetic look at Colton. "Not much of a fish person, but I'm sure it was delicious."

Jacques jumped up. "I'm going to stop Dev from eating it, if he hasn't already." He disappeared into the lobby.

"Where did you get the fish?" Joe asked, suddenly all business.

"The haddock was caught today," Colton replied. "At least . . . that's what he told me."

"*He* who?" I demanded.

Colton groaned. "Some fisherman I met on the pier. He had a hat with green and black stripes."

A hat with green and black stripes. The lobsterman Joe and I had spotted from the roof, who'd raised his hand in greeting, had been wearing a hat that fit that exact description. Could he have it out for Colton? Had he done something to the fish?

I felt a pit in my stomach that had nothing to do with dinner. If whoever was after Colton was now poisoning food . . . that meant we were all in danger.

"Listen," I said to Colton, filled with a new sense of purpose. "We've been dancing around this subject, but it's time to get real. The islanders really seem to hate you, and it's possible the fisherman did something to the fish."

Jacques had reappeared in the dining room. "The fishermen on this island are honest. Polly buys fish from them all the time, and nothing like this has ever happened."

"They aren't holding a grudge against Polly," I pointed out. "No one can deny that *something's* off with the fish, and Colton knows how to identify a fish that's not fresh, so my guess is something was added to it—something that would make us all nauseated. Not enough to really hurt us—but enough to scare us off."

Colton sighed as Jacques quietly walked back to the table and pushed his plate away. No one would meet my eyes except Joe, who seemed to be gathering himself.

"It just so happens that Frank and I have some experience

solving crimes." He paused, looking around the room. "Maybe we can help, but only if you fill us in. Is there something you're not telling us, Colton?"

The chef groaned again and exchanged a glance with Jacques.

Just as he turned back to us, Dev came running into the dining room. "Hey, guys. I don't know if it'll help, but I have some antacid and . . . oh." He stopped in the dining room doorway. "You guys look pretty bad."

"It'll be okay, Dev," Jacques said. "Come in here. Colton and I were just about to tell our guests the truth."

THE TRUTH

8

JOE

MY STOMACH WASN'T FEELING GREAT, but I tried to force down my nausea. I wanted to hear the whole story.

"My ex-wife Anika and I came to Rubble Island for the first time for an artists' retreat," Jacques began. "Anika is the painter. I was just along for the ride. We fell in love with the island—we were seriously thinking about pulling up stakes in Boston and moving out here. We couldn't imagine how we'd make a living—I worked for a travel website, and she was a teacher, but I couldn't tele-commute, and Rubble Island already had the only teacher it needed." Jacques smiled. "A few months after the retreat, Anika came running into my study with her laptop. She'd found a posting on some obscure Maine classified section:

the Sea Spray Inn on Rubble Island was for sale."

"Had you noticed it when you visited before?" Frank asked.

Jacques nodded. "We stayed here, actually. The artists were housed in the east outbuilding—that one doesn't have electricity." He raised his eyebrows. "We loved it—the history of this place. And we enjoyed not being plugged in every moment. We thought perhaps if we bought the property, we could fix it up and give others that experience. I knew about the travel industry from my job; I felt like I knew what made a hotel work. And Anika was excited to open a real gourmet restaurant here. We reached out to Polly, who was an assistant chef at our favorite bistro in Boston. She loved the idea of a change—and of making a go of island living."

I nodded, rubbing my stomach. "All right," I said. "You come out here, and everything's amazing? Then why are people throwing bricks through your window?"

Jacques's face fell. "Let me finish. At first it was hard work, but getting the inn running was rewarding. We felt like we were investing in something—building something for our future. Soon the improvements were done, the Salty Duck was open, we got some beautiful write-ups on tourist sites and in magazines. And still, we weren't making enough to pay for the work we'd done, much less turn a profit." He sighed. "Life on the island was hard, and lonely, and in the winter months, very isolating. The inn needed so much upkeep and was more expensive than we'd anticipated because of the challenges of having work done on an island. Everything had to be brought in and out by boat—the men, the supplies, the machinery. And we had to work around the ferry schedule, which in the winter was very unpredictable." He glanced sadly at Dev. "After the first year, Anika and I began arguing. First about big things, and then about every little thing. She was convinced that moving here had been a mistake. She'd envisioned a different sort of life for herself. But I wasn't ready to give up." He sighed again. "She hung in there, but eighteen months in, our marriage fell apart. We divorced, and she moved back to Boston."

I glanced at Dev. He looked uncomfortable, but not completely miserable. I figured he'd had enough time to work through his parents' divorce. It was probably just reality to him now.

Jacques cleared his throat as thunder crashed again outside, and rain began pelting the roof. "Dev wanted to stay here with me, so we worked out a custody arrangement where he was with his mother for holidays and a few weeks a year. In the summer, she gets a cottage on the mainland and Dev stays with her part of the time. In the meantime, I've tried to keep the inn going on my own, but it's been hard. For one thing, people around here really don't like change, so my proposals to bring more tourists in have been soundly rejected. But the islanders don't seem to understand—I can't keep the inn going without more visitors." He paused, glancing over at Colton. "That's where Colton came in."

Frank looked over at the chef. "Okay. How did *you* learn about the island?"

"From Polly," Colton said, lifting his chin. "We went to culinary school together, and I've always been a huge proponent of her cooking. She invited me out here to stay and have dinner at the Salty Duck. I wanted to film it for my show, actually, but we couldn't get approval for the crew." He shifted his weight. "Of course, I fell in love with the island—and with its potential. So much unused pristine land! And in the current times, the isolated location could be a plus. Who *doesn't* want to get away from it all?"

Gemma coughed. "I know *I've* been enjoying the peace and quiet."

I glanced from her to Colton. "Okay. Jacques needs more tourists here, and you love the island. What happens next?"

"One of the sponsors of my shows is Kimpton Resorts," Colton explained. "They're very high-end. They build small, all-inclusive resorts all over the world. I mentioned Rubble Island to one of my contacts, and she was very interested. She brought a team out to take a look last summer, and—well, it was a raging success!"

"A raging success how?" Frank asked.

"Kimpton Resorts has agreed to buy the Sea Spray Inn for quite a lot of money," Colton explained.

"Wait? *Buy* it?" I turned to Jacques. "I thought you just said you wanted to hang in there as innkeeper."

Jacques held his hands out and shrugged. "They made me an offer I couldn't refuse. But I've been ready to move on for a while. I've loved my time on the island, but Anika was right about one thing: we bit off more than we could chew. I learned a lot, but it's time to go back to the mainland. Dev has a couple more years of high school, and we can get him into a great school. It's time to let go."

I looked at Dev, but he was staring out the window at the lashing rain. I'd seen how much he loved the island. Knowing that he was leaving it soon had to be a hard blow.

Frank was still watching Colton. "So—how are you involved now?" he asked. "If Kimpton is buying this property, why are you so worried about the Golden Claw Awards going well? Are you just trying to help Polly out?"

Was I imagining things, or did Colton wince at the mention of Polly's name?

"Actually, as part of the deal, Kimpton wants me to take over the Salty Duck. Polly will be moving to Portland. And the inn will be expanding. . . ."

So Polly can't be thrilled about this either. "Expanding?" I asked. "How much can it expand? Most of the island is a nature preserve."

Colton coughed. "It's, erm . . . It's going to take over roughly one-third of the island."

My jaw dropped.

"How does that even work?" Frank asked. "I mean, Kimpton is building an all-inclusive resort in *Maine*? Those are usually on tropical islands somewhere. Isn't the water here, like, freezing? Can you even swim?"

"It's not for the faint of heart, admittedly," Colton replied.

"But Kimpton knows that there are lots of different kinds of travelers, and they build resorts for all of them. Not every resort is for honeymooners looking to sunbathe. This one will be more of a foodie-hiking-spa experience."

"Hiking," I muttered. "Which brings us back to the nature preserve. There must be laws about putting a development of that size so close to protected land."

Colton coughed again. "Well." He lifted a napkin to his lips and wiped his mouth. "As it happens, Kimpton's board of directors is well-connected . . . even in state government. They have every reason to believe their proposal will be approved. And it won't affect the islanders much. . . . Only three houses have to come down to make way for more cars on the island. Plus, we'll move the lobster pier and expand the ferry service to be daily in the summer."

I stared at him. "Is *that* all?" How could Colton not see that he was destroying the islanders' way of life?

Aunt Trudy leaned forward. "Is that why they've been treating you badly and why so few people showed up to help today?"

Colton sighed, looking up at the ceiling. "I suppose so."

"And we're going to put on an important awards banquet in the middle of this mess?" Aunt Trudy asked. "Isn't that maybe . . . asking for trouble?"

Colton frowned. "I suppose it could be a small problem."

"You *think*?" Frank scoffed. "No wonder you needed Aunt Trudy here so quickly!"

She glanced back at Frank, looking a little hurt.

"I mean, obviously you deserved it, Aunt Trudy," he clarified. "It's just—"

"Listen," Colton interrupted. "This is only temporary. Maybe the islanders are angry now, but when the Salty Duck lands on the cover of *Gourmet* magazine and the resort starts putting money in their pockets, they'll change their tune. *That's* why the Golden Claw Awards dinner is so important. Kimpton reps will be among the attendees, and it'll give me a chance to show them the kind of event I can pull off. We're going to put Rubble Island on the map!" He gagged and suddenly stood up again. "Excuse me," he said abruptly. "I need to go to my room."

Aunt Trudy groaned as Colton lunged toward the stairs, and Jacques buried his head in his hands. Gemma, still looking a little green, rubbed her temples.

"You guys," Frank finally said. "You're too sick to hash this out tonight. Thanks for telling us the truth, Jacques; it sheds light on a lot. But you three, go up to bed. You need your rest. Or at least, privacy."

Jacques stood up and winced, while Aunt Trudy was a little wobbly as she got to her feet. "We'll see you tomorrow," she said.

"Right," Jacques agreed, leading her and Gemma out of the dining room and toward the staircase. "And if you have any questions—"

But he instead of finishing, he gagged and raced away.

It was down to Frank, Dev, and me. We all looked at one another awkwardly.

"Well," Dev said, slumping in his chair. "Now you know my whole family sitch."

"I'm sorry about that," Frank replied. "I hope you don't think we were being nosy. I just knew something was off."

Dev shrugged. "No, man. I get it. My dad thinks he can keep this whole resort thing from blowing up, but from what I hear in town and at school, no one's willing to let it go."

I was feeling a little better, and when I glanced at my plate, I saw that I'd only eaten a small piece of fish. "You guys want to clean up? This is going to be really gross for Colton and Aunt Trudy to wake up to tomorrow."

"Good idea," said Dev, grabbing some dishes and heading into the kitchen.

"So how's it been for you?" I asked Dev a few minutes later as I passed him a plate to dry. "Your dad seems ready to leave the island, but are you?"

Dev sighed, concentrating on wiping the plate. "Well, it's been a little tough lately. The island is so small. Still, the other kids know I had nothing to do with this plan. Some of the adults are mad at my dad for selling to some big company, but mostly they leave me out of it. I just feel bad for the people it's going to affect, like Trish. Moving the lobster pier is a big deal. As for me, I'm sort of looking forward to the whole thing being over, even if it means moving away."

Frank and I made little grunts of commiseration as we finished up the dishes. I wasn't sure how I felt about Jacques selling out the island to escape a bad investment, but I *was* sure Dev had nothing to do with it.

We were finished cleaning up and about to turn in for the night when Dev suddenly stopped, staring at a corner along the kitchen's inner wall. "You guys want to see something?" he asked.

I shot a look at Frank. *You guys want to see something* is not a good phrase in the mystery-solving world. *You guys want to see something* often means a weapon or a sealed-off room in the basement with no cell service.

"Um," Frank said, casting me a wary look.

Dev leaned in and whispered conspiratorially, "Have you seen the actual Golden Claw Award trophy? It's nuts."

Oh. Well, that wasn't what I'd been expecting, and I had to admit I was a little curious. "It's here at the inn?"

Dev nodded. "It arrived on the ferry last week with an *armed guard*! Can you guys believe it? They were real disappointed we didn't have a safe to put it in. Dad finally convinced them to settle for a locked closet after pointing out that it would be pretty hard to sneak back on the ferry with no one noticing."

"I guess that's true," Frank said. "Pretty hard to throw it in your trunk and drive for the Canadian border from here."

Dev grinned. "For real." He reached for a key from a rack on the wall and gestured to a nondescript wooden door in the corner, secured with a padlock. "We put it in an old linen closet nobody uses." After unlocking and opening the padlock, he reached out and twisted the knob.

When he pulled back the door, I gasped. Even in the dark, the Golden Claw Award—shaped, surprise, like a big lobster claw—gleamed. It was bright, shiny gold, embellished with clear stones at the base.

"Those aren't *diamonds*, are they?" Frank asked.

Dev shrugged. "Beats me. It's worth a fortune, according to the guys who brought it. Winners only get to keep it for a year. Then they have to give it back."

I whistled. "It's making me nervous just looking at it."

Dev closed the door with a chuckle and locked it again.

"It's weird," Frank said as we made our way out of the kitchen. "The islanders' resentment would have made some investors tone it down—lie low, wait them out—but Colton seems to *invite* their anger. I mean, why stage this huge awards banquet on an island where everyone hates you? Why draw that kind of attention to yourself?"

Dev sighed. "I think Colton's certain he'll win in the end. But honestly, I'm not so sure he's right. I don't see the islanders coming around."

"What do you mean?" I asked.

"Let's just say, I'm glad Dad and I are getting out of here. If I know anything about the people who live here, Colton's in for the fight of his life."

A STORM'S BREWING

9

FRANK

UR FRIENDLY ISLAND ROOSTER WOKE US up again at six a.m., but this time we didn't mind. It still looked windy outside, but the rain had stopped, and the sky was momentarily clear. We took our time getting showered and dressed, then headed downstairs for breakfast. Aunt Trudy and Colton were working in the kitchen, along with the two helpers who'd been brave enough to show up. Colton's polo was gray with a bright red lobster. He looked even more agitated than the morning before. As we watched through the window in the swinging kitchen door, Colton somewhat violently attacked a zucchini with a knife, pausing to shove a thin slice into one of the helpers' faces. *See?* he seemed to be saying. *That's how you slice a zucchini!*

I wasn't sure I really wanted to go in there. After the

revelations last night, was it worth poking the bear? But Joe nodded resolutely before pushing the door open. "We have to check on Aunt Trudy."

She seemed to be keeping her distance from Colton but greeted us warmly as she continued chopping celery. "Did you boys sleep okay? How are you feeling?"

"We're fine. How are *you*?" I asked.

"Nervous. Today's the big day! But I feel much better, thank you for asking."

That was a relief. I'd felt terrible all night that Aunt Trudy had been a victim of the Bad Fish Gambit, and I hoped Joe and I would be able to figure this out before anything else happened.

As we went to grab breakfast, I noticed that Colton was now deep in conversation with Jacques. He must have come in while we were talking to Aunt Trudy.

"It's fine *now*, yes, but the storm is set to pick up again later this morning," Jacques said. "I'm just not sure they'll send out the ferry. You know they make the call in East Harbor."

"Don't be ridiculous," Colton said, juicing a lemon. "They'd be fools not to let it go out. This dinner will put Rubble Island on the map!"

Joe nudged me. "That seems like our cue to get out of here." We grabbed some blueberry muffins and juice from the fridge and brought them into the dining room.

"Wanna head to the village?" I said quietly as we ate.

"Exactly what I was thinking. Maybe we can find the fisherman with the green-and-black cap. Then once the ferry gets in—*if* it gets in—we come back here and keep an eye on Aunt Trudy and the dinner preparations."

I nodded. We couldn't be sure when another attack might happen—*if* another attack happened—but the awards banquet was definitely a big, shiny target.

"How *dare* you! I can't believe you'd show your face here again!"

Speak of the devil.

Joe and I sprang up and ran back into the kitchen. Colton was facing off with the lobsterman in the green-and-black-striped hat. The guy's face was red, although whether that was his natural coloring or he was flushed with the effort of not punching Colton, I couldn't tell.

"What're you talkin' about?" he asked, looking at Colton like he was a rabid raccoon. "I sold you my guy's best catch yesterday. Fresh as can be!"

"Your *guy's*?" Colton shouted. "I thought you caught it yourself!"

"Look, I'm a lobsterman. Lobsterman and fisherman: two different jobs. I sell my lobster around town, and I also sell fish for my buddy. I can tell you it was caught yesterday morning! Pristine stuff."

"Pristine! *Ha!* You tried to *poison* us! Every single person who ate that filth got sick. Are you trying to tell me that was a coincidence?"

The guy raised both hands. "Yes? Are you sure you cooked it right?"

Colton lunged at the lobsterman, but Aunt Trudy jumped out of nowhere and pulled him back.

"I'm an award-winning chef!" Colton panted. "Of *course* I cooked it right! I don't have time to make a complaint to the police today, but *I know what you did*, and I will do everything I can to *ruin you*. Now get out!"

The lobsterman didn't move. "Look," he said, his voice low and calm. "I'm one of the only locals who will even *talk* to you, much less do business with you. Do you really want another enemy?"

"I CERTAINLY DO!" Colton pushed past Aunt Trudy, grabbed a piece of celery off the counter, and lobbed it at the guy, bouncing it off his beard.

The lobsterman shook his head, before throwing up his hands, spinning around, and stomping out. "Have it your way!" he shouted as the door banged shut behind him.

We heard his pickup turning over, and then Aunt Trudy brushed her hands on her apron and moved back to her workstation. "Colton. *Colton!?*"

He shoved a piece of celery in his mouth. "What now?" he snapped.

"Please tell me you moved the trophy?" Looking stunned, Aunt Trudy pointed at the corner closet. "It looks like the lock was smashed!"

Colton's eyes widened. "I certainly did not." He yanked the door open, and it banged against the wall. "*No!* Nonononononononono. This can't be happening!"

I looked at Joe. Without another word, we joined Colton in front of the closet.

The padlock was gone, and the metal clasp that had held it was twisted like someone had taken a mallet to it.

And the Golden Claw Award trophy was just . . . gone.

Colton clutched at his head. "IF THIS IS SOMEONE'S SICK IDEA OF A JOKE, TELL ME NOW!"

"Look!" Joe pointed at a scuff mark on the floor by the service door.

"Joe!" I cried once we got outside. A flattened path led down the lawn toward the pier.

"Let's go."

The trail ended in front of the stone steps that led down to the pier. Clouds again covered the sky, and wind was whistling through the trees.

"Crud," a voice said behind us.

I turned to find Dev holding a backpack. "We thought you had school today."

"I do," he said, "but it doesn't start till nine. My dad is freaking out. Where do you think the thief went?"

I sighed, looking out at all the people and boats crowded around the pier. "It would make sense for whoever stole the award to get it off the island ASAP."

"How do we find out what boats left this morning?" Joe asked. "Is there a harbormaster or something?"

"On Rubble Island?" Dev chuckled. "No. The weather probably stopped most of them, but a few might have tried to beat the storm."

"They'd really go out with a storm rolling in?" I asked.

Dev nodded. "You only get paid for what you catch, and everybody's got to feed their families."

"Come on," I said. We ran toward the pier. As we got closer, we could see that the ocean was already getting rough.

Dev groaned. "I would take you guys out in the Sea Spray's boat, but it's looking too dangerous."

"Maybe Jerry at the Gull can help?" I suggested, pointing at the red cottage. "She has a window that faces the harbor. I bet she sees everything."

Inside the coffee shop, Dev ran up to the counter, where Jerry was drying some mugs. "Did you see any boats go out this morning?"

She glanced up. "Good morning to you too, kid."

"Sorry," Dev said. "It's just, this is important. It's about that awards banquet that's happening at the inn today."

"The one that's going to get ruined by the weather because Fate's on the islanders' side?" Jerry asked, smirking. "Yeah. I've heard of it."

"The award's gone missing," I explained, getting impatient. "I know you don't like Colton, but this isn't just about him."

She sighed and looked out the window. "Well, I don't doubt your story, but I didn't see any boats leave this morning."

"You're sure?" Joe pressed.

Jerry flicked her eyes from the window to Joe. "I'm sure." But something about her tone made me wonder whether she'd tell us if she *had* seen a boat leave. "Hey," she added, turning to Dev. "Did Polly tell you she got passed over for that executive chef job in Portland? They hired some old dude, big surprise."

Dev looked upset. "Yeah, I know she's still looking."

"It's real tough for female chefs, you know? Especially when you spend years of your life building up a reputation for a spot on a tiny island, and the next thing you know, your boss sells the place out from under you. She's too nice to say anything to you or your dad, of course, but I've known Polly for a long time. She's hurting."

Dev seemed to deflate a little. "Thanks, anyway."

Jerry picked up a mug and filled it with coffee. "It's not just her. The locals who worked for Jacques in the summer season—they're probably not fancy enough for the resort people. I guess they'll all have to find somewhere else to work . . . on this island ten miles off the coast."

"Listen," I said. We were wasting time. "I know you're mad about what Colton's doing with the inn. Maybe you have reason to be. But a crime was still committed here, and this awards banquet is important! For one thing, it's my aunt Trudy's chance to live out her dream. For another, if it's canceled, it might jeopardize the sale of the inn—"

"Check out that sky!" Jerry said, motioning to the window. "No boats are getting in or out. Unless Colton's guests are making the crossing right now and have very strong stomachs, that banquet's not happening tonight, whether you find that fancy award or not."

UNUSUAL SUSPECTS

10

JOE

BOUT AN HOUR AFTER WE'D LEFT, Frank and I walked back into the Sea Spray Inn's lobby. We'd dropped Dev off at school and taken the long way home, passing the pond, a small marsh, and the community garden. We'd had our eyes peeled, half hoping to spot the Golden Claw Award trophy peeking out from behind an azalea bush or something, but no dice. The sky was ready to erupt any minute. It seemed pretty clear that Colton's guests were not reaching the island today.

"Yes, hello, East Harbor PD. This is Colton Sparks, and I'm calling again about the priceless trophy that was stolen!" Colton was yelling into a landline phone in the lobby. "I'm sorry. What do you *mean* there's nothing you can do? What sort of law enforcement agency *are* you? Is this the 1800s? Am I in the Wild West?" He listened for a few more minutes, his face getting so red that I was starting to worry about his health. *"Auuuuugggghhh!"*

He threw down the phone, missing the cradle so that it dangled pathetically, bouncing on its springy cord. Colton groaned and stomped into the dining room, then through the heavy swinging door into the kitchen. I stepped forward and picked up the phone. A squawky voice was coming from the receiver. "Hello?"

There was a pause, then, "This is Chief Finley from the East Harbor police. How's it going out on Rubble Island?"

"Not great. We could use some help, honestly. Is it true that you have, like, seriously, no way to get out here?"

There was a pause. "That's correct, son. Not in this weather. As soon as the waters are safe, I'll grab another officer and come out there to investigate. Until then, well, I'd suggest trying to get some villagers to help."

"Sure," I said. *They seem to be just dying to help,* I thought.

"It's an island," Chief Finley went on. "The award couldn't have gone far. It was probably just misplaced."

We said our goodbyes and I placed the phone back into the cradle. "There's really no way for them to get out here," I whispered to Frank.

We heard whimpering from the kitchen, and when we pushed open the swinging door, Colton was in full-on meltdown mode. "It's pointless!" he shouted as he diced onions and tears streamed from his eyes. "Everything's *ruined!* The islanders have won. They always wanted me to fail!"

Aunt Trudy moved to his side and patted his arm. "That's not true. The islanders don't control the weather."

Colton sniffled. "I guess you're right. But someone did steal the Golden Claw. Anyway, it doesn't matter. I got a call from the ferry company about half an hour ago. The storm's made passage too dangerous. The awards are postponed until tomorrow, at least." He stopped to pull a handkerchief out of his pocket and blow his nose.

"That's good news, though, isn't it?" Frank asked. "It means we have twenty-four hours to find the trophy."

Colton frowned at him. "I suppose that's true, but look outside." There was a clap of thunder. Rain swirled in all directions. "Do you boys really want to search the island in *this?*"

A few hours later, my clothes were clinging to my skin. We'd borrowed slickers, but it turns out they don't do much against driving rain. Frank and I had been back to the pier, but we hadn't seen any boats coming or going, or any place where the award could be stashed.

We *had* gotten an address off a lobster boat.

"Let's think about other reasonable suspects," I said as we made our way to our destination. "I hate to say it, because she makes a mean cappuccino, but I keep coming back to Jerry."

Frank grunted. "She seems to hate Colton, that's for sure.

And she has a motive, especially if she thinks he's the reason her friends will lose their jobs."

"I didn't love how she responded to our questions this morning. She said she didn't see anything, but I'm not sure she would have told us even if she had."

"What about Polly? It sounds like she has a legitimate beef with Colton and Jacques."

I shrugged. "She seemed perfectly fine when we met her. Remember the meal she made us the night we arrived?"

"But she didn't stay for the awards. She could be keeping her resentment quiet. The food world is small, after all. Maybe she doesn't want to burn bridges with Colton."

I nodded. We'd arrived in front of 8 Black Pond Lane. "Which leaves us with this guy, the lobsterman with the green-and-black hat."

Frank looked at the house thoughtfully. "You know what's weird? He looked genuinely confused this morning when Colton accused him."

"I guess we don't know for sure that he messed with the fish. He said he sells for another guy. Who knows how many people had access to it?"

"That's the thing, though. The whole island seems to want to hurt Colton, and I can't really blame them. Let's face it—everyone on Rubble Island is a suspect."

"Well, then we'd better start asking some questions."

We walked up to the bright red door and knocked. A few seconds later we were facing the lobsterman.

"Oh, it's you boys. Listen. I don't want any more trouble. You keep your distance, and I'll refund Colton his money. I'm done with that dude."

"That's fair," I said, "but we're actually not here to talk about that."

The guy raised his bushy ginger eyebrows. "You're not? Well, what, then? It's nearly suppertime."

"The Golden Claw Award trophy is missing," Frank said.

Maybe he was a good actor, but the guy looked genuinely surprised. "Wow," he said, shaking his head. "Colton must be fuming."

"He is," Joe said."

The lobsterman sighed. "I'm Dean Bolduc, by the way."

I held out my hand. "Sorry, we should have started there. I'm Joe Hardy and this is my brother, Frank."

"Good to meet you." Dean shook my hand, then Frank's. "Look, I don't like the plans for the inn, but I tried to keep an open mind. I've come to the conclusion, though, that no one can get along with Colton Sparks. He doesn't get Rubble Island. No one deserves to get messed with, but it doesn't surprise me that someone— Hey, you guys are soaked. Do you want to come in for a minute?"

I hesitated. *Do you want to come in for a minute?* is kind of the *You guys want to see something?* of going door-to-door. It seems innocent, but it can go south really quickly. Still, I was getting a good feeling about Dean, and Frank seemed to feel the same.

"Okay," he said, before we followed the lobsterman inside.

We found ourselves in a small living room, with wood-paneled walls and an old plaid couch. A doorway on the left led to a small, warmly lit kitchen, where a woman and a little girl standing on a chair were stirring a pot on the stove. The girl waved at us before Dean led us over to some framed photos hanging on the far wall.

"The Bolduc family came down to Maine from Canada in the early twentieth century. We've been running a lobster business off Rubble Island since the 1950s." He pointed to a series of black-and-white photos of a smiling man and woman with two little boys. "This is my dad with his brother, Hank. He lives just down the block. He went away to college, and now he's the only doctor on the island. His wife's the island librarian."

"Cool," I said.

Dean pointed to another photo, this one of a pristine new lobster boat piled high with old-fashioned wooden traps. "My dad took his boat out every single morning of his life, except he took a week off once when he had pneumonia and Hank told him he'd better stay home and rest. I grew up on this island, surrounded by my dad's lobstering and fishing friends. I took lessons from the artists who came for summer retreats. I've wandered all the hiking trails so often, I know every tree and bush along every path. I know some bird families as well as I know my own neighbors."

"Wow. You're a real islander!" Frank said.

"That's right. And for us, Rubble Island isn't just a place you live. It's a place that gets into your bones. I traveled, went to school in Boston, spent a semester in Europe. I've never been anywhere on the planet as beautiful as this island. And your boy Colton wants to destroy it."

I cleared my throat. "He's not our boy, exactly. We just—"

Dean waved his hand dismissively. "Whatever. The point is, I didn't steal any fool award, but I've noticed that Colton makes enemies very easily. Maybe one of the many people he's teed off is behind making his life so difficult."

A few minutes later, not having gotten any more answers, Frank and I were back out in the rain.

"So basically," Frank said, "Dean agrees with us that everyone on this island is a suspect."

"Well, I don't think he did it," I said.

Frank nodded. "He seems pretty genuine. So that's one name we can cross off our list." He blew out a breath. "And hey, we can eliminate you and me. I feel pretty good about Aunt Trudy, too. That just leaves—"

I held up my hand. I was hearing footsteps slapping down on the wet gravel. When I turned, I let out a little gasp.

Dev was running full force up a road that led off to the right into the very dark, very wet, very muddy-looking woods. I looked at Frank. "Let's catch up to him!"

We ran as fast as we could, only slightly hampered by our heavy, wet slickers.

"What's going on?" I panted when we reached him.

"I was on my way home from school when I saw something shiny loaded into the back of a pickup truck. Even weirder, it was a truck I didn't recognize, and that's *really* rare on the island."

"Where did it go?"

"Up this road!"

"Well, let's go!"

Dev took off running again, and Frank and I followed close on his heels. It was hard to keep a steady pace in the rocky mud.

After several yards, I heard it. "An engine!" I cried. "It's can't be that far."

Frank put on a burst of speed, passing Dev and me, and I picked up the pace. I could hear Dev's footfalls slapping behind me. After a minute or two, I heard a yelp and spun around. "Dev!"

He was stuck in the mud, but he shook his head. "Keep going!" he called. "I'm fine."

Frank had turned. I wanted to help our new friend, but I also really wanted to catch whoever had stolen the Golden Claw. I exchanged a glance with my brother, and he nodded slightly. *All right. We'll keep going.* Around a bend, we came to a fork, and Frank skidded to a stop. "Do you hear the engine now?"

I listened hard, but I couldn't hear anything over the pounding of the rain. "Maybe it stopped."

Thunder crashed again, making us both jump.

"Let's split up," Frank shouted over the wind. "Yell to me if you see anything."

"Okay."

Frank went off on the path that curved to the right, while I continued on the left, concentrating in the hopes of hearing the rumble of the engine again. I tried to imagine what Colton would say if we were able to bring the trophy back tonight. Would he finally—

"*Auuugh!*" I yelled as the road suddenly dead-ended in front of a break in the trees where a cliff dropped off steeply to an inlet. The gray sea churned angrily over the rocks below.

I was running too fast to catch myself, and with the slick path, I couldn't get any traction. Panic flooded my body. *I can't stop. I can't stop!*

But I guess I was more in control than I thought. My feet skidded to a halt just inches from the edge. I let out a tiny sigh of relief, and then, just as suddenly as I'd stopped, I found myself flying forward. It'd almost felt like something had pushed me from behind.

"*Noooooo!*"

Unable to brace myself, I tumbled over the slick edge, my heart pounding. In my last moment of clarity, with the world flying past, I reached out to grab something—*anything*—and felt my fingers brush and then lock around a scrubby bush growing between two rocks. The branch was slipping, but I grabbed on with the other hand, and for the moment, it held my weight.

But not for long. I could feel the bush slowly pulling away from the rock. How much longer could it hold?

I glanced down, then instantly regretted it. The water was slamming against the cliff a good eighty feet below me. No one could survive a drop like that.

And then I felt the bush jerk.

SHATTERED 11

FRANK

"Nooooo!"

I know my brother's scream better than anybody's. And there was no mistaking, as I jogged down the muddy road that led deeper into the woods, that the person I was hearing screaming like it was the zombie apocalypse was Joe. I turned on my heel and barreled toward the sound.

I reached the fork, then pounded down the path Joe had taken. "Be careful!" another voice called from up ahead. *Dev.* I slowed, and as I rounded the next bend, I sucked in a sharp breath. The road just dead-ended.

Dev was at the top of the cliff, and as I watched, he began to scramble down.

"Stop!" I yelled, stepping closer so that I could see beyond the edge. I felt my stomach drop when I spotted Joe. He was hanging off the cliff, maybe a few yards down, clinging to a bush that looked like it would hold his weight for only a few more seconds. My heart thudded in my chest, but I knew I had to keep a cool head. It was the only way I'd get my brother to safety.

"It's too slippery," I called to Dev. "You don't want to fall too. We have to anchor ourselves to something."

I took off my belt, then scanned our surroundings until I spotted a tree—narrow enough that the belt fit around it easily, but strong enough to hold my weight. I looped my arm through the rest of the belt and then reached out for Dev. "Here. You take my hand and see if you can reach Joe."

Dev clasped my hand, then reached out his other arm. Joe leaped up, straining to grab Dev's hand, and missed. As he went back down, the bush he was clinging to dipped even farther.

"Dev!" I yelled. "Switch places with me."

Once he had me anchored, I had Dev hold on to my feet rather than my hand, then crawled on my belly, getting as far over the cliff as I could. I reached down with both hands. *Still not close enough.* Joe let out a gasp, scrabbling at the wet rocks with his free hand.

"Wait!" I cried, and pulled off my slicker, holding it tightly by one sleeve while swinging the rest down to Joe. "Grab it!"

I could feel him lunge, and then felt the welcome pull of his weight as he got a firm hold on the hood. "Got it!"

But then I heard a ripping sound. "We have to hurry!" I yelled. "Dev, try to pull me back!"

He clasped my ankles and forcefully yanked me from the ledge. Mud soaked my shirt, but I didn't care. Joe was clinging on. When I was secure on solid ground, I scrambled to my knees and pulled hard on the slicker. Soon Joe found a handhold and pulled himself up over the edge.

"That was a close one," he wheezed.

"Are you okay?"

"I will be."

For a moment we lay there panting as the rain soaked our faces and the mud coated everything else. After a minute or two, Joe raised himself up on his elbows. "Thanks, guys," he said, looking from me to Dev. "That cliff snuck up on me. Without your help, I would've been some whale's lunch."

"Whales don't eat humans," I said, slowly rising. "But I get what you mean."

"Hey, I know this might seem silly now," Dev said, after we'd all caught our breath, "but did either of you see any sign of that truck?"

The truck. Right.

"I did," I said as I unbuckled my belt from the tree. "Or at least I *thought* I did. Something disappeared around a bend up ahead of me."

Dev nodded. "Let's get out of here."

Joe picked up a big branch that was lying on the ground. He walked over to the cliff edge, paused, and then tossed it over.

Dev and I instinctively moved closer, and we all watched silently as the wood bounced down the craggy drop and hit the rocks below, breaking into a hundred pieces.

Joe shuddered.

I clapped my hand on his shoulder. "Come on."

We followed the road to the fork.

"Let's just go back to the inn," Dev suggested. "You've both been through enough."

"No, man," Joe insisted, shaking his head. "We've gotten this far. We might as well follow this truck clue to the end."

Dev sighed. "All right—if you say so."

It didn't take long to reach the point where I'd turned back. A little ways beyond that, the path curved again, and then dead-ended in front of a small log cabin. A big black pickup truck was parked out front.

"Jackpot," Joe whispered.

There was a bunch of junk piled in the back of the truck, but though I craned my neck, I couldn't spot anything shiny. "Where's the thing you saw?" I asked Dev.

He tilted his head. "There!" He pointed toward the passenger side to a bundle of . . . metal pipes. "Aww, guys, I'm sorry. . . . I led you on this wild-goose chase." He was turning back, when—

"Wait!" I called, holding up my hand. "What if the person who lives here took the award inside? Maybe we should knock." I knew I was grasping at straws, but I hated to think we'd just gone through all that for nothing.

Dev moaned. "I don't want to be a wiener, guys, but my ankle is actually really hurting now. Maybe it was the shock of the whole cliff thing. You can stay if you want, but I feel like I should get home and ice it."

I nodded. "No, of course. We'll come with you. Sorry, Dev."

"It's not your fault."

But as we headed back, I paused to look at the cabin one more time.

I couldn't help but wonder if the thief was watching me through a window.

"I'm sorry, boys," Aunt Trudy said an hour later, slipping extra pork medallions onto my plate. "I had no idea that looking around this island could be so dangerous."

I shook my head, cutting my meat. Dev had disappeared to his room as soon as we got to the inn, and Jacques had gone to check on him. Neither of them was joining us for dinner, not that I blamed them. We all could've used a rest. "It shouldn't have been. Wouldn't have been, really, if we just knew the island better."

Colton sighed and leaned back in his chair. "I suppose, for once, it was the island itself that was dangerous, not the islanders."

"Some of them feel like they have a pretty legitimate beef with you," Joe said.

"I know," said Colton. "I've heard it all before. My

beautiful resort will ruin *everything* for them by bringing tourists out here and putting more money in their pockets."

Gemma clunked down her wineglass loudly and gave him a warning look. "Be nice."

Her challenging him made me feel like I could too. "I think they'd rather keep their island than have the money you're promising. Some of the families have lived here for generations."

Colton met my gaze for a moment, then looked up at the ceiling. "I wonder if we should tweak the raspberry sauce for the panna cotta," he murmured to Aunt Trudy. "Do you think it needs more acid?"

She looked surprised. "No, it's perfect. Everything we prepared for the banquet is perfect." She shot me an apologetic look. Clearly, she'd noticed that Colton wasn't answering me, but she was too polite to point it out. She took in a long breath through her nose. "I suppose we wait and see whether there *is* a banquet tomorrow."

Rain was still pounding the windows, lightning flashing every few minutes, followed by the boom of thunder. "Is the storm really supposed to let up?" I asked. "We were out there all day. The rain didn't slow for even a minute."

Colton sat up in his chair, looking slightly sunnier. "That's one bit of good news, actually. The radio said that the storm will have a brief break tomorrow morning. I think it will be just long enough to get the boat with all the banquet guests out here."

"You can't be serious," Joe said, eyebrows raised.

"I certainly am! If there's any chance of making this awards banquet happen, I'm going to take it."

I lifted my fork. "It's just, what happens if your guests get out here, and then the storm starts up again? Doesn't that mean everyone's trapped?" *Including us. For who knows how much longer. With no police.*

Colton pursed his lips. "I'm not worried about that. We have plenty of food. It will be like a retreat! The best chefs in America, all bumping elbows in the same kitchen." He paused, looking pleased.

"But what about the award?" Joe asked. "I hate to bring it up again, but we didn't find it."

Colton nodded. "I know, but who cares about the actual *award*? It's the winning that counts." He lifted his left hand above the table and examined his fingernails. "I'm sure I can fake something about needing to have it engraved, and just give the winner a piece of paper for now. Nobody will notice."

I glanced around the room. From their expressions, nobody else was feeling quite as optimistic. But it wasn't like we had a better option. And all things being equal, it was probably better for us to have Colton focused on pulling off his coup rather than spinning out.

I watched the rain lashing at the windowpanes for a few moments. "How long is this storm supposed to last, anyway? We were supposed to go home in a few days."

Colton pushed his chair back and stood up. "Well, it's not terribly clear, boys. That's island life! You never know when a nor'easter will blow in. It may be over late tomorrow night, or it may keep going for another day." He paused. "Oh, well! We can't control the weather, can we? But you know what we *can* control? What we put on the brownie sundaes Trudy and I prepared. . . ."

THE LOBSTERS LIKE IT

12

JOE

WAS GETTING USED TO ARNOLD, THE RUBBLE Island rooster. On our third morning at the inn, we set our alarms super early and woke up before him. I was a little surprised that we hadn't run into him the day before. Maybe he liked to lie low in the afternoon.

The rain had stopped—or maybe *paused* was a better word. Dark clouds were gathered on the horizon, reminding us that this was only a temporary reprieve. "I'm glad I'm not on that boat from East Harbor today," I said.

"No kidding," Frank agreed. "I hope they brought their Dramamine."

We showered, got dressed, hurried downstairs, and ate some yogurt with granola. Colton and Trudy were still sleeping, along with (we assumed) everyone else.

Frank pushed his chair back decisively. "All right, off to the pier. With the weather changing, this might be our thief's first shot at getting the trophy off the island."

"So we'll watch the boats coming and going—"

"And if we see anything weird being loaded onto any of those boats, we'll find a way to get a closer look."

When we got down to the pier, a familiar voice piped up behind us. "Hey, dudes."

I spun around. Dev was standing there, sipping coffee out of a paper cup. "How are you everywhere at once?" I asked. "Why are you even up?"

"I come down here to get coffee before class starts most mornings. Today I'm extra early because I helped Trish get the boat ready for her mom." He pointed down the pier, where the girl we'd seen at the lobster season opening ceremony was carrying a mesh trap onto one of the lobster boats. Her long blond ponytail spilled out the back of her Red Sox cap.

After she put down the trap, she called something to the older woman we'd seen her with on opening day—her mom, I guessed—and turned back toward us. Dev waved.

"Hey, loser," she said with a grin. "Are these your friends from the big city?"

"This is Joe and Frank Hardy. They've been looking into the attacks at the inn—including that huge missing award."

She shook her head. "Yeah, that's crazy. I'm no big Colton Sparks fan either, but I'd never mess with a guy like that.

That trophy has to be super expensive, and you know he's got lawyers."

"Do you go out with your mom?" I asked, nodding toward their boat, which was now pulling off into the harbor.

She turned to follow my gaze. "Oh, yeah. I love it. That's my summer, all summer long. I can't get enough of being out on the water. I think it's in my blood."

"Seems to be in a lot of people's blood around here," Frank remarked, waving at Dean Bolduc, who was heading down from the Gull with his black-and-green hat on.

"Mornin', boys," Dean said, walking over. "Dev, Trish. Don't you have school?"

"Just on our way now, Mr. Bolduc," Dev said.

Trish nodded at me and Frank. "Nice to meet ya."

"Same to you," I said.

"What are you two doing down here at the pier?" Dean asked.

I glanced at Frank. *Hmm.* I had a feeling Dean wouldn't react kindly to us spying on the lobster boats for signs of Colton's trophy. "The truth is—" I began, just as Dean cut me off.

"You're here to look for Colton's stupid trophy, aren't you?"

"We are," I said. "If someone's trying to move it off the island, now's their chance."

Dean snorted. "You know, I've been thinking about it. I bet Colton's trying to frame the islanders for stealing his award to cheat us out of even more. These men and women getting on those boats? They're just trying to earn a living. They don't have *time* to worry about Colton and his fancy chef friends. If you boys want to understand what island life is really like, you should come out with me on my boat."

I shot Frank a glance. The dark clouds were still gathering on the horizon—a reminder that the storm would be starting back up soon. But what better place to keep an eye on the other boats than from the water? If anyone tried to ditch the trophy, we'd see it.

"You guys should do it," Dev said, startling me. I hadn't realized that he and Trish had stopped just a few feet away. "It's a pretty big honor to go out on a lobster boat. The summer tourists pay good money for the experience."

Frank's gaze flicked from the sky to the boats. But Dean was an experienced lobsterman. He'd know better than anyone when to head back to port if the weather got bad. "All right," I said. "Thanks, Mr. Bolduc. We'll take you up on that."

Twenty minutes later Frank and I were sailing between Heron and Seal Rocks out of Rubble Island's harbor aboard the *Genny*, named for Dean's mother. The *Genny*'s sternwoman, Diane, looked a little skeptical when Dean brought us aboard.

"I'm not sure you're really dressed for the weather," she'd said. "Have you been out on a lobster boat before?"

"I can't say that I have," I'd admitted.

"Well," she'd said. "I won't go easy on ya. This is your chance to turn around."

I've been kicking myself that we didn't ever since.

Not that there wasn't a lot to see. Even under a partly gray sky, the water was beautiful. Diane pointed out a group of seals sunning themselves on Heron Rock. A few minutes later Dean nudged me and pointed far off the starboard side, where a handful of fins cut swiftly through the water.

"That isn't—"

"Dolphins," Dean shouted over the boat's motor. "A whole school of them."

Dolphins. I couldn't help smiling. I hadn't even known dolphins swam up this far north.

"The ocean up here is teeming with life," Dean said. "The challenge that faces every human making their living from it is to respect that life, and fish and lobster sustainably."

"Speaking of which, we're coming up on our first traps."

Now that he mentioned it, I could see a series of dark blobs floating on the water's surface. As we got closer, I saw that each buoy had the Bolduc green and black stripes.

"How do you get them out of the water?" I asked. I realized I had no idea. The lobster traps were on the ocean floor. They weren't going to expect us to jump into the water to fish them out in March. . . .

Dean gestured to a hook, hanging off the side of the boat's cabin, which led to a winch. "It takes a little manpower."

When Diane cleared her throat, he quickly added, "Or *person*-power."

Diane steered the boat up to one of the green-and-black buoys, and Dean pulled up the rope fastened to it and attached it to the winch, then pressed a button.

"Seriously?" I asked, as the rope began to be drawn into the boat. "Is that electric?"

Dean laughed. "Yeah. We have over fifty traps, and they're each weighed down with four bricks. You think we're gonna pull 'em all up by hand?"

Soon the boxy wire trap burst from the water's surface.

"Look!" Frank cried, pointing. "You got lobsters!"

"I sure hope so," said Diane. "We need to catch a hundred and fifty pounds' worth to break even for the day."

As Dean leaned over and pulled the trap up on the railing, we could see at least four lobsters scrambling around inside, along with some smaller green crabs.

"Now we empty the trap," Diane said, putting on a pair of heavy canvas-and-rubber gloves and reaching into the pot. She pulled out the crabs first and lifted one up, dangling it by a skinny leg. It was about the size of a half-dollar, olive green, and angry. I could swear I heard it snapping its tiny little claws at me.

"These are green crabs," Diane explained. "They're an invasive species. Not edible. We throw them back."

Thwip! Thwip! Thwip! Three little crabs went back into the ocean.

"Rough!" I said.

Diane laughed at me. "You know they *live* in the ocean, right? They're probably making their way into another lobster trap right now."

She reached back into the trap and pulled out the first of the lobsters. "Uh-oh, she's a breeding female." Diane pointed to a small notch cut in the lobster's tail. "She goes back." Without further ado, she chucked the notched lobster back into the water.

"Wait," Frank said. "Who notches her tail?"

"Any lobsterman who notices a female that's a particularly good egg layer can notch her tail to warn others," Dean explained. "We all want the lobster population to stay healthy, or we're all out of a job. Lobstering was one of the first fishing industries to self-regulate. Not to brag, but now other types of fishermen and hunters look to our rules as an example of how it *should* be."

Diane had already reached in and pulled out a second lobster. "This guy looks kind of small," she said, holding up the wiggly crustacean. The lobster's shell looked blackish-green in the morning light, and it struck me how bug-like they were, especially the small ones. I remembered what Jerry had said: Whose brilliant idea was it to try to eat these things? It was hard to believe they cooked up into the delicious lobster rolls Frank and I had gotten in East Harbor.

Diane reached for something on her belt loop and pulled up a small metal measuring stick on a retracting cord.

Holding it in one hand, she spread the lobster against it with the other, pulling the claws up over its head.

"Too small. They have to be longer than three and a quarter inches between the eyes and the start of the tail, but smaller than five inches. He goes back."

Sploosh! Another lobster lived to see another day. It seemed like a good day for lobsters.

"It kinda seems like you throw back more than you keep," I observed.

"Some days it feels like that," Dean agreed. "But like I said, following the rules keeps the lobster population healthy. It's just responsible lobstering."

In the end, Dean and Diane were able to keep two medium-size lobsters from the trap. Diane placed small, thick rubber bands around their claws and tossed them into a plastic bin. Then the bait in the trap was checked, and it was closed up and lowered back down to the ocean floor.

We went from trap to trap, pulling up the pots and taking out their contents. Some traps contained nothing at all. One contained a huge lobster that we had to throw back.

"It's almost a shame," I said as I leaned over the side of the boat, watching it sink back down into the murky depths. "Imagine the size of that lobster roll!"

Dean chuckled. "The bigger they are, the tougher the meat. You're not missing much. They say the best ones, really, are the ones that've just molted. They're called shedders. Their shells are soft, so it's easy to get to the meat, but they're too delicate to ship. They're kind of a local treat."

"That's an old wives' tale," Diane said. "Give me a good old hard-shell lobster any day."

The sun was getting higher in the sky, but it was also getting harder to spot through the clouds. Still, we made our way through the traps. The work was tiring, repetitive—and also kind of beautiful. I tried to imagine a life where you had to get out on a boat and sail these waters every morning. It didn't sound like the worst thing.

"How do you get into this?" I asked. "Do you need a degree?"

"Nah," Dean scoffed. "With lobstering and fishing, you learn by doing. Most kids on the island, they start working on a lobster boat summers when they're fifteen, sixteen. You can make a decent salary as a sternman. And then when you buy your own boat, you make even more. But it takes investment along the way. You have to buy a boat and all the equipment, and keep it up."

"One problem we have on the island," Diane explained, "is keeping kids in school long enough to get their diploma, let alone convincing them to go to college. Not many of them see the point when they can make fifty thousand dollars a year lobstering at age seventeen, you know?"

I nodded. I could see a lot of benefits to the lobstering life, but it blew my mind to think some of the islanders might have never left—never lived on the mainland, even for college. It explained their fierce dedication to the place they loved.

After a few more traps, the clouds sealed out the sun altogether, and the wind began to howl.

"Uh-oh," Diane said, looking at the sky. "Storm's coming back."

Dean nodded but didn't stop winching up a trap. "It was in the forecast that it might."

Diane sighed. "Well, that was shorter than I'd hoped."

"Let's just get these last few traps," Dean said. "We're almost done."

As he and Diane began emptying the latest pot, even as the boat started lurching, I glanced up at the sky. "Is it safe? I mean, I'm sure you guys know what you're doing, but ..."

Dean grinned. "You're in good hands. You boys don't get seasick, do ya?"

By the time we'd finished with that pot and moved on to the last cluster of traps a few yards away, the waves were really rolling. Rain sprinkled down, and then it started to pound. I felt my breakfast coming up.

I ran to the other side and threw up into the sea. When I stood up shakily, Dean was watching me, part sympathetic, but a much bigger part amused. "Don't worry. The lobsters like it. You okay?" he asked. "We got some bottles of water, if you need one."

"I'll ... I'll be fine." But as soon as I got the words out the boat lurched again, and my stomach went with it. I had a feeling I wasn't cut out for the lobstering life.

I tried breathing in through my nose, out through my

mouth until the nausea passed. When I looked up, Diane was hauling another trap, and something looked super weird about it. Visibility was pretty bad, but whatever was inside there was huge, way too big to be a lobster.

And it was *shiny*.

"Wait," I said. "Is that . . . ?"

The Golden Claw Award trophy. Which somehow had made its way into Dean Bolduc's lobster trap at the bottom of the sea.

THE CULPRIT 13

FRANK

DEAN WAS FURIOUS AS WE MARCHED him up off the pier and toward the Sea Spray Inn half an hour later. Diane wanted to come with him, but Dean insisted that she wait for him at the Gull. "This is my problem. And it won't take long."

Joe was clutching the trophy like it was his baby, while the rain lashed down, soaking us even more—which I wouldn't have thought possible. If Rubble Island had taught me anything, it was that you can always be wetter.

"I didn't do anything wrong." Dean glared at me from under his cap. "If I stole this ridiculous thing, why would I invite you boys on my boat to watch me pull it up?"

"There are a lot of questions," I answered vaguely,

because honestly, he had a point. "Let's talk and see if we can figure it out."

As we pushed the front door open and stepped inside, we could see that although the lights were off, the Sea Spray Inn was a hive of activity. The lobby and dining room were full of slightly green soggy guests lying across furniture, hands draped over their eyes, moaning and generally looking miserable. I guessed that these were the chefs and Kimpton Resorts representatives in for the awards.

"Can I get anyone some coffee and a homemade bagel?" Colton asked, stepping out from the kitchen with a huge, somewhat crazed smile on his face. "We made the coffee before the power went out, thank goodness! The lox has come all the way from Scotland!"

A man half-splayed across a bench in the lobby groaned loudly. "Lox! Please, God, no."

I spotted Aunt Trudy with a tray of mugs, but no one seemed interested. She put it down on a table and walked over.

"Where were you? You boys are soaking! The power's out on the whole island. The ferry made it through, but it was storming for the last half hour, so it was a rough ride."

"I can see," Joe said, looking around.

"Jacques and Gemma are upstairs, frantically trying to get the rooms ready. I don't think Jacques really believed the ferry would make it." Aunt Trudy's eyes widened as she spotted what Joe was holding. "Is that—"

"It is," I said, raising my voice and turning toward Colton. "We found the Golden Claw!"

A flicker of irritation passed over Colton's face, and I wondered if he was angry that I'd sort of revealed that the award had been missing. He probably hadn't said anything to his fancy guests. They didn't appear to be in any state to take in information, anyway.

"You found it?" he asked as he came bounding over. "Where? What are *you* doing here?" he snapped when he noticed Dean.

"Funny story," Joe said. "Dean took us out on his boat this morning, and when he pulled up one of his last traps, the trophy was inside."

Colton's eyes bugged out and his face flushed. "I KNEW IT!"

I reached out before he lunged at Dean, who looked more bemused than scared. "Wait, wait, wait. It's more complicated than that."

"As I have explained to these boys," Dean said, "if I wanted to steal your silly trophy, it would be uncommonly stupid of me to put it in a lobster trap and then haul it up with them watching."

Colton sputtered. "Maybe—maybe you didn't want to get away with it! Maybe you wanted to make a *statement*, just like that brick through my window and poisoning my fish! Yes, you're very big on *statements*, aren't you?"

I could hear murmurs from the guests. It surprised me a

little that Colton had mentioned the brick and the fish in front of them.

Dean was clearly reaching the end of his rope. He threw up his hands and backed toward the door. "Look, the last time I checked, you folks aren't the police, which means you have no power to hold me. I'm going home to take a shower. We can figure this out later."

"Hold it right there," Colton called. "You're not going anywhere!"

"Try and stop me!" Dean faked like he was going to lunge at Colton. It was enough to send the celebrity chef shrinking back.

"You're being a bully!" Colton shouted. "You're showing your true colors!"

"*I didn't do anything to you!*"

Clearly, we needed to break this up before it came to blows, but should we let Dean go home? If he really was behind the trophy theft and the harassment, it was pretty much guaranteed we wouldn't see him again. Even with the storm, Dean knew enough about the island—and enough sympathetic souls—to disappear for a while. And even when the police could get out here, *if* they could, I had trouble imagining them going after a lifelong islander on the circumstantial evidence of a celebrity chef.

Even knowing that, I was inclined to let Dean be on his way. As he'd pointed out, it simply didn't make sense for him to steal the award, only to reveal it right in front of us.

And he'd been nice to Colton—nicer than any of the other islanders. It could have been a long con to get Colton to trust him enough to slip him the bad fish, but I doubted it.

"Kimpton Resorts bought this inn fair and square!" Colton yelled. "Who are *you* to tell me what I can and can't do with my talent?"

"Talent!" Dean scoffed. "I once watched you put olives in a lobster roll! *Olives!*"

"Frank." Joe put the Golden Claw down on the floor and nudged me. "Little help here?"

Colton was mounting a spirited defense of "vinegary notes" in lobster rolls when the door behind us opened, accompanied by a curtain of rain. "Oh—um, hi? Everyone?"

Colton cut off his tirade abruptly as all eyes turned to Dev.

Dev always seemed to show up at just the wrong time, didn't he?

Or just the right one.

"What are you doing home?" Joe asked. "It's barely noon. Does school get out for lunch here?"

Dev shook his head. "No, I wish. They sent us home since the electricity's out."

"Oh, right." Joe nodded. "I forgot."

"Wow. You found the award!" Dev said, grinning as he took in the shiny statue on the floor. "Wild! Did something weird happen to it?"

"Well," Joe began, "we went out on Dean's lobster boat,

like you suggested. And then the storm broke again, and then . . ."

An idea had formed in my mind. As Joe continued with his story, I pulled my phone out and glanced at the screen. "Gosh," I said loudly, "I hate to interrupt, but I need to call my mom back about our cat's medicine right away, and my phone is almost dead. Dev, can I borrow yours?"

Dev looked from Joe to me. "Uh . . . I guess so? If you can get any service." He reached into his backpack and handed me his smartphone.

"Thanks, man. Excuse me for a minute." I ignored Joe's *what the heck* face (we don't even have a cat) and walked to the door that opened from the dining room out to the covered porch. At the last minute, I turned and called casually, "Oh, I'll need the pass code."

Dev looked caught off guard. "Oh, I can just—"

"What's that?"

Dev sighed. "One-four-eight-three-one-three."

"Thanks, dude," I said before stepping outside. It was still cold, wet, and windy. I huddled in a corner far from the eaves, where I unlocked Dev's phone and clicked through. Colton and Dean were still screaming at each other inside, with Dev interjecting every so often. After a few minutes, I heard Jacques's voice join the fray.

"Stop it! Stop it right now! No fighting in my inn!"

There it is! I felt a thrill of satisfaction as I saw what I'd been looking for. I pushed open the door just in time to see

Jacques holding back Colton while Joe had a hand around Dean's forearm. Trudy and Dev were ushering the chefs and Kimpton reps up the stairs to their rooms. It looked like it was going to come to blows any minute, and I didn't like Colton's chances.

"*STOP!*" I yelled. "Dean's right. He's got nothing to do with this! The person who stole the trophy is—"

Slam! I looked at the front door and the empty space where the culprit had been standing.

SEVERAL RECKLESS THINGS

14

JOE

"—DEV!"

Dang. I really hate it when Frank beats me to figuring out a case. But I have total faith in my brother, so when Frank announced that Dev was behind everything that had happened at the Sea Spray Inn, I didn't question it. Wordlessly, I bolted after Dev, Frank behind me.

Outside, the storm was still raging—the sound nearly deafening. It was hard to keep my bearings. Even though it wasn't even noon yet, it was as dark as dusk.

"Come on!" Frank called, gesturing to a set of soggy footprints through the soaked lawn that led to one of the outbuildings.

We ran up two low steps and pulled open a weathered wooden door. Inside, it was pitch-black. Frank yanked out his phone (which had plenty of juice) and turned on the flashlight feature. It didn't give off much light, but it was enough to make out a long hallway with doors opening off to either side. Old-fashioned glass lamps lined the walls, but we didn't have any way to light them. Wet shoe prints led down the hall.

"Do you hear anything?" Frank asked as we crept along.

"No." It was kind of creepy how Dev seemed to have dematerialized. But I was sure, from the tracks we'd seen, that he was in here somewhere.

Thunk!

Frank and I both looked up at the ceiling.

"There must be stairs in here somewhere," I whispered.

Frank crept ahead, sweeping the light back and forth along the walls. At the end of the hallway, to the right, steep wooden steps led in both directions.

We crept up to the second floor.

A window at the far end of the passageway provided a little more light, but the silence and the thin layer of dust that covered everything made it just as creepy.

"Look," I said, gesturing to the floor. Footsteps in the dust led to a door across the hall, closest to the stairs. We tiptoed over, pausing for a moment before I grabbed the old-fashioned doorknob and then, with a nod from Frank, twisted and shoved the door open. I'd secretly hoped it would be locked.

It swung hard and banged against the wall.

But when we raced inside, we found—

Nothing.

Well, not nothing. There were two narrow twin beds with white coverlets, two nightstands, and an antique wooden dresser. Gas lamps were mounted on the wall, a closet held extra blankets, and a bare-bones bathroom opened off to the side. Through two small, multipaned windows lashed by rain and wind, I could see the storm was still howling away.

But there was no Dev.

Thud!

Frank perked up. "He's downstairs! Did you hear that?"

"Yeah, but *how*?"

"There's no time to worry about it. Let's go."

We retraced our steps into the hall and down the stairs. Back on the first floor, we paused and listened.

Bump.

The noise had come from the other side of the wall we were facing—the room closest to the stairway.

We rushed to the door and pushed it open, making an effort to be quieter this time. Less light seemed to reach the windows on the ground floor. We heard a gasp, and then another thud. Frank aimed his flashlight ahead and we entered the room.

"Dev!" I called. "Just come here, man! We can work this out."

But when Frank aimed his phone all around the small

room—there was nothing. I ran to the closet and pulled it open, but found only more blankets.

"What the heck is *happening*?" I moaned. "Is he *magic*?"

"No," said Frank calmly, still bouncing his flashlight around. "He just knows more about this place than we do."

He flashed the light to our right, then took a step closer, focusing on one small section of the wall. "Look."

Sure enough, when I peered closer, there was a small square cut into the wall. It would have been easy enough to overlook. At the bottom was a handle.

Frank walked over and touched the handle, then pushed it up. I gasped. The tiny door retracted into the wall, revealing a small wooden shaft.

"A tiny elevator?" I whispered. "For your mouse guests?"

Frank shook his head and lowered his voice so I could barely hear him. "It's a dumbwaiter, dumbbrother." He flashed his light down the shaft, then leaned in. "I'm guessing this leads to the kitchen. *That's* why these rooms are so small—I bet when the inn opened, they weren't guest rooms at all, but servants' quarters or little prep rooms for food service." He flashed the light above his head, up into the shaft. "He's above us," he whispered. "From the look of it, I think he's on the third floor."

"Huh?" I asked.

Frank leaned back and closed the little door, then gestured for me to follow him into the hallway. "This inn was built before elevators were common, Joe. But this was still a fancy resort, and people expected to be fed. There's a kitchen somewhere in this building—I'd guess the basement. They would prepare meals there, then put them in the dumbwaiter to haul them up to the guest floors, where a servant would bring them to the guests."

I stared at him. "Okay. And Dev is . . . ?"

"Upstairs," Frank said. "The mouse elevator, as you call it, wasn't below us. And it looks farther than one floor up—so he must have ridden it to the third floor. He's been riding back and forth between rooms in the dumbwaiter to try to throw us off. We're going to have to trap him."

"How?"

Frank looked thoughtful. "I'm going to stay here on the first floor. If I were Dev, while we were distracted, I'd get out on the ground floor and jet from the building. We'll have to scare him into moving."

I raised my eyebrows. "And that's my job? The scarer?"

"Who's as scary as you, Joe?"

I puffed out my chest. "No one."

"Try harder!"

I growled.

"Who has the worst jokes?" Frank asked.

"Now that's just insulting."

"Right. Anyway, what you'll do is . . ."

Frank and I worked out our next steps, and then I began making my way up two flights of stairs—none too quietly.

"I dunno, Frank!" I said, loudly enough to be overheard,

but not *so* loud that it would be obvious I was playacting. "How does he manage to stay one step ahead of us? It's like magic."

I lowered my voice slightly and tried to become—how can I say it?—60 percent geekier. "Well, funny you should ask, Joe," I said, doing my best Frank. "I have a theory, and that's . . . *that he's climbing down the outside of the building!*"

I reached the top of the stairs, pulled out my own phone, and turned on the flashlight. I spotted the first room across from the stairway—the room the dumbwaiter would open into—and switched my voice back to normal. "But Frank! There's a storm out there! Do you really think—"

Frank's voice: "He's lived at this inn for years, Joe. He must know this building like the back of his hand. *Unlike us.*"

I walked right up to the door we suspected Dev was hiding behind. "Let's check this one, Frank."

Frank's voice: "Good idea, Joe."

Turning the knob, I pushed the door open, tiptoeing in like I still was trying to be sneaky. But I could tell my message had been received, loud and clear, when I heard a slam, then a squeaky sound coming from the wall.

Dev was on the move downstairs. That meant *I* needed to be too.

I ran back down the stairs to the ground floor, trying to be as quiet as possible.

I slid into the room downstairs just as the door to the dumbwaiter creaked open.

"Aha!" Frank cried, shining his flashlight into the tiny elevator—and *right* into Dev's eyes.

Dev looked panicked. He grabbed the dumbwaiter's ropes and started tugging.

"Don't bother," Frank warned him. "Joe can be upstairs to meet you wherever you decide to go."

"Come on out of there," I suggested, trying to keep my voice light. "Don't freak out, man. We can figure this all out."

Reluctantly, Dev unfurled himself from the tiny wooden platform, dropping down with another *thud*.

"I didn't do this," he insisted, looking desperately from me to Frank. "Why would I? My family is the victim here! Why would I endanger my dad's deal by harassing Colton? He was *thrilled* to sell the inn!"

"He was," Frank said in an even voice, "but *you* weren't thrilled about it. You love this island. It was obvious the day you showed us around. You know every path, every tree, every beautiful vista. You've spent a big chunk of your childhood here, and you don't want it to change."

I thought about that. As usual, Frank was right. Love for Rubble Island radiated off Dev. Why had it never occurred to me that he might want to stop the move so much that he would do something reckless? Or really, several reckless things.

Dev lifted his chin. "You can't prove that."

"Actually, I can," Frank said, pulling a second phone out of his jacket pocket. "Your text messages are more than enough proof. I guess Trish was in on your plan too, huh?"

Dev seemed to deflate a little. "Is she gonna be in trouble?"

"We don't know," I said. "We'll have to see."

Dev frowned.

"I'm guessing you slipped out of the inn the night we arrived to throw the brick through Colton's window," Frank said. "We hadn't even met you then."

Dev looked out the window at the rain.

"You had access to the fish Dean sold Colton, too," I added. "You're working on an independent study about food science. When you went into the kitchen to get a drink, I'm sure you could have distracted Colton just long enough to add something to the fish to make us sick and throw suspicion on Dean."

I tried to catch Dev's eye, but he wouldn't look at me.

"And of course," Frank said with a sigh, "you had access to the trophy. You showed us where it was, which was pretty gutsy of you, now that I think about it."

Dev snorted and shook his head.

"Then you smashed the lock to throw further suspicion onto the locals, and stole the trophy," Frank continued. "You must have hidden it when you went to school, and then you and Trish snuck out on her mom's lobster boat to plant the trophy in Dean's trap."

Dev sighed, still staring out the window. Frank moved around to face him. "That's not the worst thing you did."

Dev's gaze flicked up for a moment. Then he let out a

sound that was like a moan mixed with a whimper. "I didn't mean it," he whispered.

"What?" I asked, feeling lost.

"When Dev realized that we were looking into the case and we were serious about it, he got scared," Frank explained. "He tried to get rid of us, sending us chasing after that truck. He faked hurting his ankle so we'd go on ahead without him. He knew we'd split at the fork in the road, just like we did."

A horrible thought occurred to me. I'd almost forgotten the feeling of thinking I'd caught myself, only to go hurtling over the edge. *Of course.* Suddenly Dev seemed less like a cool kid we'd been hanging around with all week, and more like a monster.

Dev focused on the floor and whimpered again. That was all I needed to know I was right.

"My guess is that Trish was waiting by the cliff to push you," Frank said, looking at me, sympathy in his eyes. "And I *also* guess that Dev's plan was to follow me and incapacitate me once they'd finished you off, Joe—but you yelled for help, and I came after you instead."

I was speechless. The image of the branch I'd thrown over the cliff shattering on the rocks below played over and over in my mind. If Frank hadn't pieced everything together, who knew what Dev might have done to us before the week was out?

Dev hunched over. He didn't look like he could stand much longer.

Frank moved a little closer and reached out to touch

Dev's shoulder. "I know, deep down, you must be a good person. You had another chance to let both of us fall when we tried to save Joe, and instead you lashed yourself to that tree and helped get us to safety. And that's how I know it'll be okay. We won't—"

Out of nowhere, Dev sprang back to his full height, slamming his shoulder into Frank's nose hard enough that I could hear the impact. Frank fell back, moaning, and in the confusion, I lurched toward my brother and Dev ran straight past, out the door.

Frank was clutching his nose, which was bleeding pretty hard. "I'm okay!" he cried. "Go!"

But just as I turned to follow his command, we heard the front door crash against the wall. Dev was gone.

I bolted down the hallway after him. Thunder crashed as I stumbled down the steps to the slick lawn, and then a flash of lightning followed, momentarily blinding me. In the aftermath, I saw Dev's silhouette racing toward the road Frank and I had taken the first night.

"He's heading to the pier!" I yelled at Frank. We tore across the lawn, slipping and struggling to stay upright, then slammed onto the gravel road.

"Where's he going to go?" Frank shouted. "He can't . . ."

But his voice trailed off as we watched Dev run down a ramp to the docks. At the bottom was a small motorboat with wide benches and a steel canopy. Printed on the side was THE SEA SPRAY INN, RUBBLE ISLAND.

"Dev told us the inn has a boat," I reminded Frank.

"Crud," he muttered. "The inn has a boat."

By the time we reached the bottom of the ramp, Dev had jumped into the boat, unwound the dock line, and started the engine. The waves were already tossing the craft violently from side to side, and we could see he was having trouble just staying on his feet. Thunder crashed again; it was hard to see through the driving rain and the mist it brought up from the sea.

"*Dev, stop!*" Frank hollered. "*The storm! It's too dangerous!*"

Dev paused just long enough to shout back, "*Come on! I'm not stupid! I know how much trouble I'm in!*"

The boat jerked away from the dock, rolling violently.

"*No!*" Frank yelled, pointing toward the harbor. I followed his gaze. A giant wave had formed between Heron and Seal Rocks and was just cresting—and Dev was headed straight for it.

We watched, stunned, as almost in slow motion, the boat smashed into the wave and capsized, and Dev was slammed under the churning water.

STORM'S END 15

FRANK

HAT THE HECK'S GOING ON?"

"That fool!"

As Dev slipped below, I heard voices behind us. Several people from the inn, including Dean, Jacques, Trudy, and a few of the banquet guests, must have seen us follow Dev down here. As I watched, Jerry and Diane ran out of the Gull.

"What happened?" Diane yelled, eyeing the rolling surf.

"It's Dev," Jacques replied, panicked. "He fell in!"

Dean struggled out of his jacket and threw it down onto the wooden pier. Before any of us could stop him, he took a running start and then leaped off the edge, falling twenty feet into the churning waters.

"No!" I yelled.

158

But Diane had made her way to my side. "Don't worry," she said, whipping off her own jacket. "If anyone can pull him out, it's us." And then she ran and dove into the water too.

Those of us left on the pier ran to the edge to get a better view. At first I could only see Dean's soaked head, but then Diane popped up about ten feet away. They swam against the waves to where the boat still rocked angrily, now on its side.

Dean's head disappeared under the water while Diane clung to what I guessed was the boat's dock line. While the waves were rough enough to push her head under a few times, she always resurfaced, gasping.

Dean's head finally bobbed up, but as soon as he spotted Diane, he shook it. She called something to him, and they switched places. Thunder crashed as she disappeared below the surface, and a bolt of lightning split the sky. When she emerged a minute later, she'd had no better luck.

Jacques let out a moan. Jerry put her arm around his shoulders, murmuring something into his ear. He wiped at his eyes and nodded.

Dean dived again. This time it took him longer to resurface. I glanced at Joe. It would be horrible to lose one life from this island; it would be unthinkable to lose two.

Diane seemed to be getting restless. She was ducking down while still clinging to the dock line, trying to spot Dev underwater, I guessed. After what seemed like forever, a wet head emerged from the rough surf.

Dev's!

A few seconds later Dean's head followed. He yelled to Diane. She let go of the dock line to swim over and help support Dev, who I realized was unconscious. Fighting the surf, clearly exhausted, they swam back over to the pier and then around to the docks, where together, they heaved Dev out of the water.

As Joe and I ran down the ramp, Diane and Dean were struggling to get out themselves.

"It's okay!" I yelled. "I know CPR! Let Joe and me take care of him."

For a few minutes, I was aware of nothing but Dev's heartbeat (still strong) and getting air into his lungs. It felt like forever before Dev suddenly lurched up and coughed, leaning over and spewing a mouthful of seawater. He groaned.

I heard applause from the pier. Half the village was now gathered there, but Jerry moved to the front with Jacques.

"Nice job, Hardy boys!" she shouted. "Now let's take him to my apartment and warm him up. I have EMT training—I can check him to see if he needs medical attention."

It was sort of impressive how many people managed to jam into Jerry's small one-bedroom apartment off the side of the Gull. Dev was conscious, but he wasn't saying much as Jerry built a fire in the fireplace, and Jacques bundled him in handmade quilts.

"I'm so glad you're okay," I heard Jacques say, his voice trembling, before wrapping Dev in a big hug.

After a few minutes, Dev seemed to come back into himself a little more. "I'm sorry," he croaked. "I'm just so sorry."

"Tell me what happened," said Jacques gently. He was sitting in a chair opposite the couch where Dev had been laid out. "I knew you had doubts about moving, but I had no idea you were so against it that you'd go to these lengths. It's one thing to steal a trophy, Dev. But you tried to hurt people!"

"I know." Dev shook his head again, closing his eyes. "I just . . . I got scared when I realized how deep in I was. I didn't set out to hurt anyone. I just couldn't imagine what Colton wants happening to Rubble Island."

"You can say that again," Bill scoffed.

A red-haired woman wearing an expensive-looking shawl and black pants stepped forward. "Listen, my name is Darcy Voss. I'm general manager of Kimpton Resorts' Northeast division. I just wanted to say, we knew there was some opposition to building a resort on Rubble Island, but we really didn't realize how deeply it went, for some of you." She glanced at Dev.

"How could you not realize?" Jerry asked, shaking her head. "Colton and you Kimpton people want to change *everything* about our home!"

Darcy winced. "The resort would require only small changes to the infrastructure—"

Bruce Fenton broke in. "You only think the changes are small because you've never been here. Our island is close-knit and beautiful. It works for the people who live here, and it's a little challenging for people who don't, and that's how we like it. We don't *want* more cars or more ferries or less preserved land. With all those changes, Rubble Island wouldn't be Rubble Island anymore."

Colton was looking increasingly uncomfortable. "But with the new resort, Rubble Island could become a premier destination! You wouldn't just get a four-star restaurant. . . . Who *knows* what would come here if the resort is a success? High-end shopping! Investment in electricity, cell service, roads! Rubble Island could become a place you barely recognize!"

"Don't you get it?" Bruce asked. "We don't want a place we can't recognize! This is our home, and we love it the way it is!"

Darcy glanced at a couple of people who flanked her, one eyebrow raised.

"Listen," said Jerry, "nobody else is going to hurt anyone to make their point." She shot a look at Dev. "However, I can say with confidence that none of the islanders will *ever* be on board with this resort. And so you may get what you want, but it will come at the price of angering a whole lot of people, and never quite feeling welcome in the place you've completely upended."

Darcy let out a sharp breath through her nose and nodded.

"Thank you for that insight. I mean that. Let me go outside and have a word with some of my colleagues."

When she opened the door, I realized the storm was finally blowing itself out. The rain was slowing, and I spotted a patch of sunshine in the distance before the door closed again.

Jacques looked around at his neighbors. "Listen, I have some regrets about the way this all happened. I saw an opportunity for my family and I took it. But I realize now that I was putting my own desires ahead of everyone else's. I do wish I'd thought more about what the resort would mean to the island." He glanced at Colton. "I guess, in a way, I heard what I wanted to hear."

Dev sat up. "Maybe it's not too late! Maybe it can be undone and we can stay?"

Jacques looked at his son and shook his head sadly. "I'm sorry, Dev, but the answer is no. I'm very concerned about some of the things you did to manipulate Colton. At the very least, you need to talk to someone who can help you more than I can. We need to leave Rubble Island—but maybe we can stay close by in Maine."

Dev looked down into his lap, clearly disappointed, but nodded.

After a few moments of silence, the door opened and Darcy and the other Kimpton representatives walked back in, shooting an awkward look at Colton. "I'd like to make an announcement," Darcy said loudly. "I've had a chance to discuss this unique situation with my team, and based on what we've seen today, how difficult it was to get to the island, and what you're all saying about your opposition to the resort—we're thinking about adjusting our plans. Perhaps Kimpton can still buy the inn but scale back our footprint, involve the island residents more in our planning."

A cheer went up from the islanders in the apartment.

Darcy went on, "It appears that it takes an . . . unusual tourist to feel at home here. Perhaps not our typical resort customer. But even in this weather, it's clear: there is much beauty here."

"You can say that again," Jerry replied. "Let's make sure we keep it that way."

Colton was shaking his head. "But how will this work? What about our agreement? I can't have a five-star restaurant on an island with a few hundred residents and a small inn!"

Darcy looked at Colton and nodded slowly. "Yeeeeeeah. Well, maybe that's better for everyone," she said calmly. "I'm sure we can find some way of honoring our agreement that wouldn't be quite so risky and disruptive. I understand this Polly person is very popular at the Salty Duck. Maybe we could look into keeping that in business and open a Colton Sparks restaurant at one of our other locations."

Colton sighed deeply and crossed his arms. "What about the one-of-a-kind menu I've put together that combines local seafood and produce with the hottest food trends out of New York?" he demanded.

Darcy tilted her head. "I expect that will have to be amended."

Colton threw up his hand, sputtering. "W-well, maybe we should just cancel the Golden Claw Awards! If my food isn't—"

A familiar voice cut through the chatter: "WE MOST CERTAINLY WILL NOT!"

Aunt Trudy stepped out from behind Diane and stared Colton down. There was no anger in her gaze, but it was clear she wasn't going to change her mind. "We worked hard on this banquet! All the food is ready! And this was my prize, Colton—I earned it!"

Colton sighed again. "But no one cares about my food!"

"*I care* about your food," our aunt insisted. "I learned so much from you in such a short amount of time. Everything I believed about your talent is true. And no matter what happens on Rubble Island, nothing will ever change that. You're a genius, Colton! And now it's our chance to show everybody."

Colton looked down at the floor, then back at Aunt Trudy. He shifted his weight, then smiled. "All right," he finally said. "I hope all of you are hungry, because the Golden Claw Awards are on for tonight!"

THE GOLDEN CLAW

16

JOE

LTIMATELY, THE GOLDEN CLAW AWARDS aren't about one place or restaurant," Colton said into the microphone behind the small podium that had been placed in the Salty Duck's dining room. "They're about a way of life. An appreciation for everything the sea gives us, and all the people who work so hard to bring it to us. I'm thrilled today to present the Golden Claw to an up-and-coming chef I know from the YUM! studios in New York: Saachi Chahal!"

An Indian woman stood in the front of the dining room, beaming, and began to make her way to the podium. Colton handed her the giant recovered trophy, then made a little joke, pretending he wasn't going to let go. Saachi laughed and finally claimed the award.

"I'm so honored," she said. "From the beginning of my career, I've been drawn to the subtle flavors of the ocean...."

Frank poked my arm. "Did you try the lobster casserole?" he asked. "It's pretty freaking killer. I wonder if they used one of the lobsters we caught?"

I laughed. "Maybe. I'm not sure whether Dean and Colton worked things out in time."

Frank looked up, then gestured across the room. By the door to the kitchen, Colton and Aunt Trudy were chatting quietly. Her eyes were crinkled up as she laughed at something he'd said. She looked happier than I'd seen her in a long time.

"I should take a picture," I said. "Aunt Trudy will want to remember her time with Colton. My phone's charging upstairs. I'm going to run and get it."

I pushed my chair back and quietly made my way to the door to the lobby, which had been covered with a heavy velvet curtain. Really, the Sea Spray Inn looked fancier than I would have thought possible. I wasn't prepared for what I saw when I pushed through the curtain and opened the door.

Dev and Jacques were at the front entrance, speaking to two uniformed police officers, a man and a woman, whose uniforms read EAST HARBOR PD. I almost cried out, "They finally made it!" but now clearly wasn't the time. Dev's friend Trish hovered behind the officers, flanked by a middle-aged couple who must have been her parents, looking like she couldn't believe what was happening.

". . . very serious charges," the female officer was saying. "We're here to escort you both to the mainland, where you'll be questioned by a detective. Then we'll decide whether to make an arrest."

Dev looked nervous, but Jacques patted him on the shoulder. "Don't worry. We're in this together."

I moved forward, and Dev's focus fluttered to me. If I'd been worried that he might be mad at us for unmasking him, the fear in his eyes told me it didn't matter anymore. And anyway, Frank and I had done the only thing we could have. I reminded myself that Dev and Trish tried to hurt us, even if Dev had changed his mind at the last minute. They needed help.

"Hey," I said, nodding at him. "Honestly, Frank and I wish you well."

"Thanks," Dev said, though his voice was barely audible. I walked past him up the stairs to my room. When I went back through the lobby after grabbing my phone, the whole party was gone. *It's the East Harbor Police's problem to solve now,* I told myself, and headed back into the Salty Duck.

"This is simply the best octopus salad I've ever had," a middle-aged man with a handlebar mustache said as I passed his table. "Colton really is a master of seafood!"

Saachi Chahal had gone back to her seat and was chatting with her tablemates, her face flushed with pleasure. As I settled back at my own table, Colton patted Aunt Trudy on the shoulder—I snapped a quick picture—and walked up to the podium again, tapping the mic.

"Excuse me." The chattering in the dining room quieted, and all eyes turned to Colton, who leaned into the mic.

"I just want to say that I wouldn't have been able to pull this off without the help of a very special person: Trudy Hardy. She came into my life because she won a contest on the YUM! Network, but I can honestly say, she is one of the most gifted home chefs I've ever met, as well as one of the kindest and warmest people. This week was our first time working together, but I'm sure it won't be the last. Please, join me in toasting Trudy!"

Everyone raised their glasses, including me and Frank. Aunt Trudy was blushing, but she nodded at the room graciously. "To Trudy!" everyone shouted.

The next afternoon Frank, Aunt Trudy, and I dragged our suitcases back down to the pier and boarded the public ferry to East Harbor. Colton had left on a private boat that morning. Aunt Trudy said he'd offered her a job at his Kimpton Resorts restaurant, whenever it got up and running. "Of course I won't take it," she said as we stood on the top deck, watching Rubble Island recede into the distance. "I could never leave you boys and your parents. And I'm much happier being a home chef, I think—there's less pressure that way! But I'm sure Colton's and my paths will cross again."

I smiled. From a distance, we could see the lobster boats sailing back into the harbor after a long morning spent pulling traps. I thought I spotted Dean and Diane on their boat, and I waved wildly, but we were probably already too far away. "Well, our time on the island was pretty dramatic, but I'm really glad we got to visit."

"Definitely," Frank said. "Rubble Island is beautiful, and in the end, the islanders proved to be pretty good people."

"Yes," Aunt Trudy said. "I hope things work out for Dev and Jacques."

"Me too. And I hope things work out for Colton," Frank said. "He seemed better by the time we left, but I know he was upset to lose the opportunity to open a restaurant on the island."

"I think he'll get over it," Aunt Trudy said. "When he said goodbye, he was already talking about launching a new concept in Santa Fe. He asked me what I knew about Hatch green chiles and promised to keep in touch."

I looked at Frank and smiled. It sounded like Aunt Trudy was right. Colton wasn't really gone from our lives yet. *Great.*

Rubble Island grew smaller and smaller in the distance, then disappeared altogether. About twenty minutes after we'd left the pier that faced the Gull, the mainland came into view, and soon we were sailing toward the village of East Harbor. I hoped we'd be received a little more pleasantly this time around.

"We should pick up some lobsters when we get to town," Aunt Trudy mused. "The lobstermen will pack them to travel, you know. Colton showed me the most interesting recipe...."